Death in the Watchhouse

Death in the Watchhouse

Ed McKie

©Ed McKie 2018

ISBN:978-1-9804-4661-3

J E

Jeaned Books
Warrington, Cheshire. UK

Previously in this series.

Death in a Museum

1

The porch of the old watchhouse in the corner of the churchyard of St. Mary Magdalen was barely twenty inches deep but Constable George Morrison took shelter there anyway. According to the newspapers this March of 1862 had been the wettest for fifty years. This George was prepared to believe. It seemed to him his cape had not been dry since Christmas.

His friend and fellow-lodger, Frank Evans, a newspaper reporter ran along the street and joined him in the porch. "Thought it was you, George." he said: "Although you all look alike in the dark."

George just sniffed, ignored the remark and asked: "So where have you been at this time on a Saturday night?"

"Visiting a young lady if you must know. Would not be out on a night like this otherwise."

Frank fished in his pocket for a packet of cigarettes and matches and turned into the lee of the doorway to protect the flame. As he did so he leaned against the heavy wooden door which moved against the pressure and the padlock in the hasp fell open.

This surprised George as the building had not been used for at least thirty years. As far as he knew there would be no reason for anyone to go into it and leave the padlock unsecured. Previously the watchhouse was the base for the parish watchmen before the introduction of the police service. Built as a basic stone structure with a strange octagonal shape it sat in the corner of the churchyard of St. Mary Magdalen. The churchyard was no longer used for burials but even so superstitions locals did not linger in the vicinity after dark.

It was a matter of moments to ease the rusty lock off the hasp and push open the door. Pitch black inside and the bull nose lantern did little to illuminate the interior. There was just sufficient light to see the body of a man lying not far inside. A matter of moments to establish the man was dead and the lantern also showed a serious injury to his head. George went outside retrieving his rattle from his inside pocket and used it to summon the constables on the two adjoining beats.

Several minutes passed before the first arrived who was then dispatched to the police station in the Borough High street. He had to notify the inspector of a particularly brutal murder. When the second constable arrived George suggested he should go to Guy's hospital to see if he could bring a doctor along in case there was anything that could be done, but he doubted it. George was in no position to tell the constable to do this but his colleague accepted, for the moment, George was in charge and agreed it would show initiative to be doing something.

Frank Evans, unable to put aside his newspaper man's instincts, took the opportunity to examine the body even in the poor light provided by the police lantern which the departing constable left behind.

He could see the man was fairly well dressed, about five foot six or seven inches tall and perhaps of middle age. The injuries to the head appeared to be confined to the back of the skull but it was difficult to ascertain more in the poor light.

Sergeant Brewer arrived on the scene with two extra constables and several lanterns in order to illuminate the scene inside the watchhouse. He approved of the actions taken by Morrison so far but thought calling a doctor was not really necessary.

The man was dead so he could have been taken directly to the mortuary at St. Thomas' hospital. Might as well now wait for the arrival of Inspector Brannan who would no doubt like to see the circumstances for himself. The doctor however arrived before any further action could be taken. A grumpy man who also agreed his journey in this weather was unnecessary. Attempting an examination of a corpse in the gloom of the watchhouse would serve no purpose. The doctor departed as the inspector arrived.

Inspector Brannan, a career policeman born into a police family was also not amused at being called away from home to look at a body. Reluctant to criticise the Sergeant for having called him but was of the opinion it was not necessary. A murder during a robbery was not unusual and Brewer should have been able to deal with it himself.

"Right, carry on Brewer, get the body taken to the mortuary and we will look at the circumstances in the morning. Not much more to be done at this time of night in the dark"

The trundle cart from the police station arrived and the body unceremoniously bundled into it.

"There is not much more to be done here, tonight" said Brewer, parroting the inspector, "I will go back to the station and send a padlock to be put on this door. When it is done, continue with your patrol but keep a sharp lookout, although at a guess this body has been here for a couple of days, so it is unlikely whoever did it is going to be hanging around now."

Turning to Frank Evans, trying, unsuccessfully to be inconspicuous, "You are the newspaperman aren't you?"

Evans agreed.

"So what are you doing here?"

"I saw the constable in the doorway here and stopped to light a cigarette, the padlock fell open as I did so and I came in with the constable and saw what you saw yourself. A dead man on the floor with his head bashed in with something heavy."

"Well then, as a witness you will need to stop being a newspaper man and it would be helpful if you did not publish this story until you hear about it officially."

Frank Evans knew better than to argue with the sergeant, even though he knew there was nothing the policeman could do if he went and published the story. But being a weekly, his newspaper was not due to be published again for a few days, so it was a moot point. Also it would not be politic to sour the reasonably friendly relations he had with the police in the Borough as they often supplied stories, even unintentionally.

Brewer marched off like the former sergeant major he was. Evans resumed smoking his cigarette and Morrison continued to examine the scene as best he could by the light of his lantern.

There was still evidence of the use for which the building was erected. A small cell occupied one corner and the rest of the room was simply furnished with a rough wooden table and two benches. The old watchmen were not intended to stay in the watchhouse they were to be on their rounds of the parish from dusk to dawn, irrespective of the weather. They returned only if a miscreant was apprehended and needed locking up for the rest of the night before being taken before the magistrate in the morning.

With the body removed, George was able to observe the blood on the floor from the head wound which indicated the murder might have taken place in the room. He couldn't imagine what the man was doing there. Years of accumulated dust on the floor and heaped into the corners, cobwebs festooned the walls and every projection and little light came through the window on this moonless, miserable night.

"Well what do you surmise, detective?" grinned Frank Evans at his companion.

"I am not surmising anything. I am looking at whatever evidence there is here, which is very little"

"Come then, what little do you see?" pursued the newspaper man.

George paused to gather his thoughts.

"Well, stating the obvious, first there has been a murder, second it took place here, third there is no sign of a struggle, therefore the attacker took the victim by surprise and finally if the third point is true then the two men knew each other as this would then be an arranged meeting."

"Nothing else?"

"This building is passed at least once every hour, during the night, so at least one of the parties was familiar with this area in order to be able to go into the building and arrange for the other to do so. Admittedly it would not take many days to establish, but it would need to be confirmed before arranging the meeting. This padlock has not been forced so a key was used to open it but for some reason it was not locked on leaving, only pushed closed. Perhaps an interruption or a passerby. The porch here is not deep and as you know does not provide much in the way of shelter and by the same token no cover either for any ill-doing."

"Well your new padlock has arrived, so I will bid you goodnight. You continue your watery rounds, whilst I sleep the sleep of the just in the dry."

George ignored his friend's cheerfulness, accepted the padlock from the constable who brought it, locked the door and then needed to decide whether to keep the key or to send it back to the station. He was not sure why but he decided to put the key in his pocket and resumed the perambulation of his beat.

The rest of the night passed without incident and although the rain died away he did not receive the customary check visit by the sergeant nor inspector. There was no need for a return to the station until the end of his shift at six o'clock in the morning. Night shift patrols in this division were considerably shorter than on the day shift. At barely two and a half miles long and at the regulation pace, he would normally pass each point every hour.

He was not due to go back on duty until the following morning as this was the last day of his night duty shift and his next roster was to be at the desk of the police station during the day.

He managed to sign off at the station and having written up his report of the discovery of the body in the watchhouse escaped without being given extra duty which often happened at the end of a shift. He was tired so returned immediately to his lodgings, a cup of tea and a few biscuits and went to bed.

2

Being awakened at noon by a knock on his door, he growled "come in" half expecting it to be his fellow lodger, Frank Evans. the newspaper reporter, but it turned out to be one of his colleagues from the police station. "Sergeant Brewer says you are to return to the station at one o'clock" he reported with a grin.

"What on earth for? I am not supposed to be back on duty till six o'clock tomorrow morning"

"Dunno" the constable replied, "Didn't say, and as he had a mood on, I didn't ask. Leave it with you then" and whisked out of the door as fast as his cumbersome boots would allow.

These changeover days were a nuisance as far as meals were concerned. Coming off night duty early in the morning and going to bed without a meal invariably resulted in George waking with a ravenous hunger. On the days he ate breakfast, it usually comprised some cups of tea or coffee and some slices of bread, toasted over the gas ring in his room.

Today he decided an early dinner at the chophouse would be preferable in view of his summons to the station. Without knowing why he had to go to the station he could not even guess when he would be returning to his lodgings.

With less than an hour before needing to be back at the station it was going to be a quick meal, so George opted for a meat pudding.

This business of being regarded as being available twenty-four hours a day was one of the things which irked George about being a policeman. And it was totally unnecessary. It was true the station was short of the official complement, but there were still close to two hundred constables in the division so there was no need to be called out of bed less than six hours after going off duty. He sometimes thought sergeants had a perverse streak in their natures which made them enjoy calling men in for duty in these circumstances.

3

A little after one o'clock Morrison went into the station just off Borough High Street and went to the sergeant's office. Brewer looked meaningfully at his pocket watch but said nothing.

"You wanted to see me, Sarge."

"Yes, there is a job for you."

"But I'm not on again until tomorrow morning"

"I know that, but this will not wait until the morning, there's been time for a good sleep, so it won't hurt you to get a bit of fresh daytime air as you've been on nights for two weeks"

George was still to be convinced the daytime air in Bermondsey was any cleaner than the night time, if anything it would be dirtier. There were no stinking horses about at night and the factories were not belching out as much smoke. Admittedly the smell from the breweries and the tanneries never went away but he knew better than to argue the point with Sergeant Brewer, an ex-army man who expected to be obeyed without question.

Brewer resumed his instructions. "The coroner is holding his inquest tomorrow on the corpse you found last night. It's lucky he doesn't work on a Sunday, otherwise it would be today. We don't know who the cove is so we need to be able to tell the coroner we have made enquiries. The artist has made a drawing of the face as well as he can and I want you to go round the local pubs and see if the publicans can give us a name, and if we are lucky an address."

George looked at the drawing and was doubtful if anyone was going to be able to recognise the corpse from it. Admittedly his view of the face was by the light of his lantern in that dark room and perhaps the lights in the mortuary enabled a reasonable impression to be made. In any case, this drawing was a face which could fit hundreds of the men moving around the streets of Southwark. Talk about a needle in a haystack!

Still, there was no choice nor any plan for that matter. Where to start? There were close to a dozen public houses within a stone's throw of his beat and twice as many within two stones throw. And what if the man was not from around here but was inveigled into the area in order to be murdered? There was even a greater chance he was a visitor to Bermondsey and murdered during a robbery so would not be known in the area.

Anyway, there was nothing to be done but to commence this hopeless task. Despite Sergeant Brewer's optimism in the matter, George did not feel he was fully rested after a twelve-hour shift on his feet for most of the time. His beat around this part of Bermondsey did not include many places to shelter from the rain, let alone sit down to take the weight off his feet. Even the places that could be stopped in, few and far between as they were, could not be used for any great length of time as there was always the possibility the sergeant would appear from nowhere, as it were, and even worse the inspector was also inclined to take it into his head to walk around with the sergeant. "Keeping the constables on their toes" was the motivation they were told, but keeping them off their arses was much more like it. George never fully understood, even after all this time, why the upper echelons of the police service regarded it as such a crime for a constable to take a few rests during a twelve-hour shift. They surely knew that for most men it was physically impossible to perambulate the beat for this time without a break. They would know of course, but for their own, undisclosed purposes, they pretended it was not so.

So off he went.

4

It was not that he didn't do the job properly, but George was not surprised he found no one who could identify the face of the man in the drawing. Pub after pub, being offered drinks as he went, there being the assumption it is what he was really calling in for. It was not that George did not enjoy a drink, it was he was scrupulous in not accepting drinks for fear of feeling he was under some obligation to the publican.

George completed the rounds of all the local pubs by five in the afternoon and returned to the station. There he handed the drawing of the dead man back to Sergeant Brewer and advised him he was unsuccessful in finding anyone who admitted to knowing the man. Brewer was tempted to tell the young man to go and get some tea and then go out again and visit all the other pubs in the area but reluctantly accepted this was probably a wild goose chase and he will have to advise the coroner the man was unidentified. This may not be a problem, numerous corpses are fished from the Thames every year, many unrecognisable because of injuries caused by fish and passing river traffic so they remained unclaimed and unrecognised. Generally, the coroner accepted this and advised the jury to record an open verdict on an unknown person. The police did not have the resources to follow up every unidentified corpse, so the coroner's verdict was the end of story unless some relative turned up later, but when they did it was mostly too late the body having been disposed of to the dissecting room at the hospital for the education of the medical students.

George gratefully returned to his digs and decided to spend a quiet evening indoors with a book purchased recently from a second-hand bookshop.

His hopes for a quiet evening were dashed when a little after seven his neighbour Frank Evans knocked on his door.

"Good evening detective" he greeted.

"If you are going to continue to use this stupid name then you can close the door behind you and not bother knocking on it again."

"Don't be so grumpy George. You should be fully rested from your day off."

George considered that he was entitled to be grumpy and rounded on his friend. "I did not get a day off. I'm a policeman, working for twelve hours every day with a short break when I change from the night shift to the day shift. It is not really a day off and even less so when, like today, I had to go to work anyway."

Frank pulled up the only other chair in the room and asked: "Was it to do with your body?"

"Well of course it was. They made a drawing of the corpse and although there are close to two hundred constables working from the Borough police station there is only one capable of taking the drawing round all the pubs in the area to see if anyone could recognise him"

"Ah well then, serves you right for being the only one who can read and write decent English and is capable of using his own brain."

George was not to be mollified by this brazen flattery "So what did you come here for."

Frank stood up "Well not to talk to someone so out of sorts with his job he doesn't know how to be pleasant to a friend who is not responsible."

"I'm sorry Frank. Didn't mean to be rude but it does sometimes get to me that working a twelve hour day is not enough. The one day break between day and night shifts doesn't exist as far as the service is concerned. The inspector goes home to his wife every evening, stays away on Sundays and doesn't think a lowly constable is entitled to time off with his family."

"You don't have a family."

"Of course I have a family, my parents are still alive, but I was thinking more of the married men who do have children that they rarely see and spend little time with. Being a policeman should not entail giving up a family life."

"I agree" responded the newspaper man, "but there is nothing you can do about it, so why not let me cheer you up by buying you a couple of pints. Slip on your own clothes and we will go down to Camberwell or even up the West End where nobody knows you and enjoy ourselves? What about it?"

George was not in the mood for such junketing, however agreed, if Frank wished, they could go to their usual chophouse for a meal with a couple of pints of porter to wash it down.

Frank Evans was more keen on his own suggestion but agreed.

Of course being a newspaper man Frank was unable to resist bringing up the subject of the body after they started on their first pint and ordered the meals. Although his meal in the middle of the day had satisfied him at the time he was still a healthy young man and the exercise of the job meant he was always hungry.

"So do you really know nothing about this cove in the watchhouse then?"

"No I don't and I don't think anyone at the station does either. There was no identification on the body, no purse or money so the guessing is he was robbed, but why shove the body in the watchhouse? That wasn't necessary for a simple street robbery in the dark and it couldn't have happened in the daylight."

"Why so?"

"Because there are always too many people about for goodness sake. So an attack in daylight without being seen is very difficult to achieve."

"Well that's true, but as you say if it took place at night with no one around why bother to hide the body. Robbers don't do that do they?"

"Not usually and in any case. most robberies don't result in the death of the victim, so it may not have been that. Difficult though to imagine a motive that makes any sense. Street attacks are common mostly of the snatch variety with a quick make off into a side street. "

"So what if it was not a robbery then?"

"A meeting turning to violence? Possible but then why nothing in the pockets? That's why it doesn't make any sense."

The reporter continued with his meal and George hoped it was the end of that conversation. He was not averse to these discussions with his friend, but when there was not enough information about the subject to come to any conclusions he easily got bored. He liked detective stories in fiction and read avidly but it was not easy to translate them to the real life of a police constable in Bermondsey.

But George was not really surprised when Frank finished his meal and returned to the subject. Having obviously been conning it over in his mind whilst he ate.

"Right then. Logically it was not a robbery but a private matter and the murderer decided to make it look like a robbery by removing all the possessions from the pockets. This would also make it more difficult to identify the body. The murderer then made the mistake of hiding the body in the watchhouse not realising a robber would not do that."

There was no option for George but to go along with the discussion and add thoughts of his own to counter the points being made by Frank.

"Logic. as you say, suggests no robbery but a cover-up. But there is another possibility. What if the murder actually took place inside the watchhouse? Then it is not a question of hiding the body it is already there. Removing the possessions then indicates it was simply an attempt to delay the identification of the victim rather than feigning a robbery."

"Well if that is true then it clearly indicates there is the fear the murderer would be implicated once the name of the victim is known."

The constable agreed but demurred that this was all conjecture and was not really productive.

Frank Evans would not be put off but called for a second pair of pints of porter.

"OK, I realise that I view these matters from a different stand as a newspaper reporter. You think you can only deal with facts which of course is true whereas I look at the same facts but need to make them into a story. This means that I need to conjecture about the meaning of the facts and I consider, and have said in some of my reports, police inspectors would do a better job of dealing with crimes if they did the same."

"But Frank, your criticism would only apply if we were always dealing with mysteries. The average police inspector rarely has to do that. Most crimes are straightforward, the crime is seen, the victim is known, the perpetrator is seen and for the most part. is known. These then are the only facts necessary to take a case before a magistrate and eventually to the Bailey if it is sufficiently serious. So there is no need for speculation about the why of a fact. It is there and that is that."

Frank quickly responded because this was a subject he thought about a great deal. He was not anti- police, in his job he could not afford to be so. But it was his opinion there were insufficient senior officers of inspector and above in the police force who had been policemen themselves. The detective branch based at Scotland Yard was not very good at detecting crime and appeared to concentrate on averting crime by watching and often instigating crimes by known criminals in order to catch them in the act.

"I grant you do need to deal in facts and so does your inspector. But it seems to me, and I spend a lot of time in the police courts and around the stations on this side of the river, quite often not all the facts are gathered in. Enough to get a conviction and that is that. I often think the whole story is not given to a magistrate because the inspector does not know the whole story because he does not ask. You know yourself many cases sent to the Bailey end up with an acquittal."

George agreed this was often the case but was not aware it presented a problem to the police service.

"Of course its a problem for the police service" the reporter resumed. "Its a waste of time and money for a start and taking a criminal to the Bailey, who is clearly guilty but who gets off for lack of evidence reflects badly on the police and has a knock-on effect on later cases in the same court."

"What on earth do you mean?"

"I've seen what I suspect has been a knock on at the Bailey. A case is dismissed and the same policeman whose evidence was doubted appears in the following case. The Judge looks at him and immediately doubts him again. Don't forget most of the acquittals at the Bailey are on the Judges instructions because the evidence has not been good enough."

George agreed but pointed out that mostly there was not sufficient evidence available and the police had to rely on witness testimony which often changed when they get in the witness box in court under pressure from a defence lawyer. This was not the fault of the police.

Frank was forced to agree and the subject was dropped and they discussed other subjects for half an hour or so. George returned to his lodgings and Frank resumed his quest for entertainment in other places.

5

George was back in the station before six o'clock in the morning to start his stint on the front desk. He was to remain until eleven o'clock when required to attend the inquest.

The inquest hearing was a brief affair. George had attended a few inquests since joining the police, but only in Southwark, so was unaware what happened elsewhere. But the inquests conducted by the Southwark Coroner, who also held the same post for the City of London seemed to be almost perfunctory.

George gave evidence first and described finding the body. The doctor who attended in the night was not called, but Doctor Lewis from St. Thomas's Hospital had carried out the post-mortem and gave a detailed and gruesome description of the injury to the victim's head. An iron bar or something similar was the most likely instrument of death. He was of the opinion the death had taken place at least two days previously and possibly three so Wednesday was more likely than Thursday.

Sergeant Brewer gave evidence that the identity of the victim had not been established but enquiries were still being made. The coroner decided to adjourn the inquest for seven days and moved on to the next inquest, a young girl found drowned in the Thames.

Frank Evans was in the room and remained for the following inquest. George left to return to his desk at the station and surmised there would be a verdict of suicide before he got back into the street.

6

George noticed as he got back to the station that the drawing of the dead man was on the noticeboard close to the entrance with the usual caption "Do you know this man?"

Considering most of the people who came into the station of their own accord could neither read nor write, it was unlikely to get a response.

In the early afternoon a burly, well-dressed man came into the station and paused in front of the drawing before approaching the front desk. "Is Inspector Brannan in today, Constable?"

Morrison was unsure if it was wise to admit to knowing who the enquirer was or to feign ignorance. He decided there was no harm in adopting the former course and responded "Yes Mr Brannan, he's in and as far as I know is alone, so there should be no problem if you go straight through. I am sure you know the way."

Brannan nodded and made his way to the back office.

James Brannan whilst an inspector with the Metropolitan police specialised in the catching of coin forgers. As a result of his success, he was now employed in that capacity by the Royal Mint. He was also the father of the current Inspector at the Borough police station, but the regular visits of the coining expert to the station were rarely for personal reasons.

Brannan knocked on the door and on hearing a "come in" entered and spoke first.

"Good afternoon Inspector "

They adopted this style of addressing in a police station or other official venue, to keep their private and official lives separate.

"Good afternoon Mr Brannan, what can I do for you?"

"Well, to be honest, I originally came about a small coining couple operating in Magdalen street I thought you could watch and picked up when you can get some evidence. It is only small scale as far as I can establish but they need to be got off the streets sooner rather than later.

However on coming into your station, I noticed a drawing of a man you are enquiring about, what can you tell me about it?"

The inspector outlined the finding of the body and the result of the inquest.

"Do you think you recognise this man?"

The older man hesitated for a moment and then admitted he thought that he did.

"I would need to see the body, of course to be sure, but I think so."

"In connection with coining?"

"Yes, but there is no evidence, just suspicions about something larger in scale than we have been used to, but he has been watched. I will go and see the body and then check up with the watchers to see when they lost sight of him."

The inspector knew his father's activities spanned the whole of London so asked. "Is he from around these parts or the other side of the river?"

"Well up until now he has not been seen in Southwark, but as I said I will need to see the body before spending any more time on your corpse. If it is not the man I am speaking of then it has nothing to do with me."

Inspector Brannan got up, "I will accompany you to the mortuary, as a civilian they may put obstacles in your way."

7

The mortuary at St. Thomas's hospital was only a five minute walk from the police station so father and son only spoke of family matters on the way.

The mortuary attendant found no difficulty in producing the body for a uniformed inspector of police and whoever was accompanying him.

The body was stored in a cold room awaiting instructions from the coroner, but now being at least a week old was beginning to smell.

The signs of the post-mortem examination were obvious but the damage to the head was insufficient to obscure the face. "It certainly looks like the man I saw a few times but can't be one hundred per-cent certain. I don't have a full description of him so at the moment have no means of knowing if there were any distinguishing features which would allow a positive identification. I will speak to my watchers to see if they know any more and if necessary, with your permission, I will send one of them down to view this body. I will admit I hope it is not my man as he was my only lead in an important investigation."

The inspector turned to the mortuary attendant and asked: "What happened to his clothes?"

Without replying, the attendant went to a cupboard in a corner of the room and produced a bundle of clothing tied around with a piece of rough cord. There was no hat.

"Did your man always wear a hat?" he asked the man from the mint, "I see his hair is thinning so would expect him to be a hat wearer."

"Yes he was wearing a billy-cock each time I saw him, but I can check on that."

"I wonder why he took it off to have his head stoved in?"

Turning again to the attendant he asked: "Is there a copy of the post-mortem report here?"

"Yes sir, there are two, but I don't think I am permitted to give them to you."

"I do not want to take them away, only to look."

A sheaf of papers was produced covered in almost illegible handwriting.

"Are both copies in the same hand?

"No sir, the other is a copy."

"Then give me the other in the hope I can read it."

He was fortunate, the second bundle of papers were in fair copperplate script.

Quickly scanning through the sheets Inspector Brannan found what he was looking for. "The doctor was of the opinion the weapon was an iron bar or something similar. We found nothing like that at the scene or nearby the following morning."

"Any distinguishing marks mentioned?" queried the other.

"No mention of anything, no tattoos, old scars or deformities. We can see for ourselves this is not a working man, no callouses on his hands, nails well trimmed and relatively clean, quite decent clothes and boots. Not a nob but not hard up either. So where is that hat?"

It was apparent little more could be learned by looking at the body so they prepared to leave. A final word to the attendant.

"Please make a note in your book we have been and that I request no further examination or dissection of the body take place without my first being informed at the Borough Police station."

The attendant assented and the pair left, parting at the entrance to the hospital with Mr Brannan promising to keep the inspector informed and to try to arrange with someone more familiar with his suspect to come to view the body.

8

George Morrison was again at the desk of the police station when Mr James Brannan presented himself with another man.

"Is the Inspector in?"

"No Mr Brannan, he is at a division meeting. Sergeant Brewer is here"

The Sergeant appeared, almost as if summoned.

"Sergeant, I spoke with the inspector yesterday and told him I may be able to help identify your dead un from the watchhouse. Perhaps he told you. My colleague here is more familiar with the man we think it might be, so I would be grateful if you or a constable could accompany us to the mortuary to see if we can be certain."

"Yes sir, he did mention it. Morrison here can come with you so there should be no problems with you both viewing the body."

Morrison should not have been taken by surprise, but he was. As an old army man and used to giving orders Brewer naturally delegated everything.

This was George's first visit to the mortuary even though it was on the same level of the hospital as the museum where a couple of years previously he dealt with an apparent suicide.

The body was produced and the man accompanying Brannan immediately agreed it was their suspect.

"Are you sure, Tom"

"Yes, on the right-hand side of the face, above the beard is a small mole with two pock marks below under the eye. It makes a kind of triangle and I have sat a few evenings across a room from this cove and would recognise that arrangement anywhere. This is definitely Da Silva"

"When was the last time you saw him?"

" Close to six weeks ago now. He dropped out of sight as it were and I found he left his lodgings in Princes Square the same day. His landlady said he told her he was coming to live in Southwark and got a room near Admiral Square. Two men were sent over to this side of the river to try to pick up the scent, but the address was a false one, so it was necessary to bide our time for something more positive from other avenues."

"For crying out loud Tom, there has been time for you to get a handle on the man on this side of the river in four weeks"

"I agree, Mr Brannan, there has been time but not the men. You know how overcommitted we are with the number of investigations in hand with too few men to cover them all. You remind me constantly we are not the police, which unfortunately is true. We are doing police work with a less men."

"This is not the place for this discussion."

Turning to Morrison he suggested he should take the bundle of clothes worn by the dead man back to the station and examine them for any indication of where the man might have been living.

George was aware the former inspector knew this was the right thing to do, and said so to the attendant, who again produced the bundle and George signed in his book for them.

"You will notice there is no hat. Mr Findlay here agrees with my recollection that this man always wore a billycock. So it has gone missing. Might be important, may be not. Please tell Inspector Brannan I will send him full details of what we know of this man by tomorrow."

George knew the surname of the man, but that was all but thought if it was quiet at the station this afternoon he would take it on himself to examine the clothing.

9

Back at the station, George resumed his duties at the desk and passed on the message from Brannan to Sergeant Brewer who would relay it to the inspector when he arrived.

George took a break in the middle of the day for a cup of tea and a couple of slices of bread after which he decided to examine the bundle of clothing from the body at the watchhouse.

It was unexceptional apart from the bloodstains. A quite good quality pair of button boots but which had not been cleaned for some time and a pair of knitted socks. The trousers were dark brown rather than black, of a worsted material. The shirt was cotton and there was a neckerchief which as tied more like a cravat, Morrison recalled.

The waistcoat was double breasted with nothing in the pockets, but the wear on one of the lower buttonholes appeared to indicate there had regularly been a watch-chain attached.

The overcoat was single-breasted, nothing in the pockets, not even a handkerchief. There was no tailor's label but George knew it was originally expensive. That meant nothing of course, the trade in second-hand clothing was probably one of the largest commercial activities in London. It was not only the working classes and poor who clothed themselves in previously owned clothes, tradesmen and shopkeepers did the same. On the death of a member of the family, many upper-class households disposed of unwanted clothes by passing them on to staff who then sold them on to the dealers. So good quality clothes had a class system of its own.

There was nothing to be learned from this sad bundle and he began to fold up the clothes when noticed what appeared to be a thickened section on the edge of the coat. Closer examination made it clear there was something sewn into the edge fold.

"Sergeant. There is something you need to see in the dead man's clothes," he called through the door of the office.

Brewer grumbled but came out anyway.

"What have you got?"

"Something in this lining here Sarge."

"Let's see what it is then"

Brewer produced a fold-up knife from his pocket and used the blade to open up the seam close to the slight bulge in the coat. This produced four coins. Half-crowns and brand new by the look of them but the date was ten years earlier so they had not been in circulation.

"Forgeries, Sarge?"

Morrison was already linking this find to the interest of Mr Brannan, the investigator for the Royal Mint, in the dead man.

"I shouldn't think so" Brewer replied, "Or if they are, they're very good".

A quick spin of one of the coins on the counter indicated they did not ring true.

"Curious this, don't you think constable? Mr Brannan interested in our dead man who has got some very good forgeries on his person but nothing else"

"Very curious Sarge. Part of a gang fall out perhaps but made to look like a simple murder for robbery. And where is his hat?"

"What do you mean, where is his hat?"

"No hat Sarge but Mr Brannan's man said their suspect always wore a hat. So where is the hat? Wasn't in the watchhouse and not in the churchyard. No one would take their hat off in that cold dreary watchhouse just to hold a conversation. And would a deliberate murderer take the victim's hat off before bashing him on the head and then wear the hat as he went off? Doesn't seem very likely."

"You read too much Morrison. Anyway this clearly makes this a job for the inspector, not you and me thank goodness. Wrap all this up and put it in the inspector's office, no doubt he will be along shortly"

10

Ex Inspector Brannan left his house in Finsbury at 7.30 in the morning and began to walk towards London Bridge. He was a reasonably fit man, despite his age and walked most of the time when about his business for the Mint. His work often made his fitness useful when taking part in an arrest as there was no inhibitions about using force when necessary. As a civilian he should only have observed arrests being made, after laying information with the local police station about coining operations, but old habits died hard.

It was a fine morning so he enjoyed the walk and soon arrived at the Borough Police station.

Once again, George Morrison was at the desk so he greeted him and told him the inspector was in his office and indicated he was expected.

"I'm afraid Inspector, there is very little more I can tell you about Da Silva that will help with your enquiries about his death. What little we know of him is confined to only the last six months when he appeared on the scene in St. George in the East, almost from nowhere, at the same time some very clever forgeries began to appear."

"Like these?"

And the inspector threw the two coins found in the lining of the dead man's coat onto the table.

"Where did you get these?" the older man responded.

"Hidden in the lining of the coat."

"Why weren't they found originally?"

"Because they were well hidden sewn into the lining of the coat."

"They should have been found."

"That's easy to say. There was no reason to have searched the clothing the first time round, and in any case, they were at the morgue. There was nothing in the pockets, so there was no reason to think this was other than a robbery gone wrong. Even now, these coins do not give any evidence it was not that. We didn't know this man was your coiner and any robber is also unlikely to have known it either."

"Well we don't know Da Silva is the actual coiner, but he is involved, of that we are certain."

"So what is the source of these very expert forgeries?"

"We don't know that either. The experts at the mint think they are made in quite a sophisticated way. Not the usual impression in plaster of paris filled with cheap alloys that will only pass muster to a half-drunk barman in a dark pub on a Saturday night. These are good, not quite true and have even been paid into banks without being noticed amongst a handful of genuine coins. So the blanks are good, able to be used many times in a mechanical manner and the metal is almost full weight, but not silver of course?"

"Have the experts at the Mint any idea about the method of production?"

"No, but they think it is mechanical and could even be a scaled-down version of the machinery in use at the Mint itself. They find it difficult to comprehend, of course, but cannot come up with any other suggestions even though the power required for such an operation is not normally available outside of a factory."

"Imported, do you think? Da Silva is not an English name."

"Probably not genuine either. We have thought about the possibility of importation but the numbers involved suggest otherwise or there is a very clever system of dribbling the fakes onto the market in small numbers. This would imply a larger organisation than we have been able to identify."

"So what about this man's associates? Can't you have them pulled in to Scotland Yard for questioning?"

The man from the Mint paused whilst he lit his pipe and perhaps to give himself time to consider how much he should reveal to the inspector.

"It's rather more complicated. At the moment I am unable to say any more, but I have to attend a meeting at the

Mint this afternoon about these forgeries and after that, you may well hear more. This meeting this afternoon will be attended by the Governor of the Bank of England himself as well as people from the Home Office. I am going to drop this information about the death of the principal suspect in and no doubt there will be repercussions. I have some inkling of the suspicions in the Home office about the forgeries but have no idea how they will react. There are only two possibilities, of course, they will want a full investigation, no doubt by the detective branch or they will want it swept under the carpet in order not to prejudice the tracking down of the forgery ring if there is a ring. You will have to wait and see, but in the meantime perhaps it would be wise to continue with whatever you have been doing. You now know who the man is, or claims to be, we cant be certain Da Silva is his real name or that he was using that name in Southwark. But it gives you something to go on. Here is a copy of the drawing we made whilst he was still alive but it is not necessarily any better than your own artist's efforts."

The inspector nodded his agreement of his father's assessment of the situation knowing it would be useless to press for more information. Perhaps it would be better not to know too much and to continue with the enquiries as if he did not know.

The older man rose, they shook hands and he departed.

11

Inspector Brannan usually remained at the police station until after the shift parade at 6 pm before going to his home at Camberwell Green.

He did not live in the division but near enough to get back if anything serious arose requiring him to return.

The parade was taking place but the inspector was in his office when the door opened and the Superintendent walked in without knocking. He never considered he was required to announce his presence in the police station.

"Good evening Inspector," he said taking the chair in the corner of the room. This was another of his habits to assert his authority, if not superiority. He would not sit in the chair in front of the desk whilst the inspector sat in his own chair. If he arrived at the station whilst the inspector was out, he would seat himself behind the desk and remain there until he left, even if the incumbent returned in the meantime.

Brannan was used to these little foibles. The Superintendent was another of the former army officers holding senior positions in the Metropolitan Police, who could not shake off the old military habits.

"Now then Brannan, what is happening with this murder last weekend. Have you arrested anyone yet?"

"No Superintendent. We have no suspects so cannot arrest anyone."

"Well, what are you doing then?"

"We are doing what we always do in these circumstances, Superintendent."

Brannan was well aware the Superintendent knew about the Mint connection, or he would not be asking his questions in this way. He obviously wanted to know how much Brannan knew before revealing his own information.

"We have only today, confirmed the identity of the victim. This has been supplied by the forgery team working for the Royal Mint. Apparently was under surveillance for some time in the east end as either a suspected forger or as a middle-man. It seems he slipped out from under their noses some weeks ago and came to this side of the river. So far we have not identified where he was living if in fact, he was living in the division. You no doubt saw the two shifts being shown the drawings that we have to see if any had come across the man on the beats. I have not heard from the Sergeants as yet if it was successful, but I do not hold out too many hopes.

If it was not, I will have one of the drawings re-engraved and copies made so all the beat men on the day shift tomorrow can take them out with them and show them around as widely as possible. Until we know where the man was living on this side of the river then we will not be able to identify what he was doing in or near the watchhouse"

"Do you think he was involved in any coining in the division."

"I have no means of knowing Superintendent. In the past, this part of the division has only ever had small- scale coining activity. Most of it not very good and easily detected. Mr Brannan, however, believes that what this man was involved with was more sophisticated, and this was perhaps confirmed by the four forged coins found hidden in his clothing."

"Do you still have these coins?"

Brannan did not reply. He went to the small safe in the corner of the room and retrieved the coins, handing them to the Superintendent before resuming his seat. He always found it difficult to retain his composure when faced with the abrupt manner this superintendent adopted to all lower ranks.

"The certainly seem very good Brannan."

"I am not an expert on forgeries, but Mr Brannan says the experts at the Mint think they are amongst the best they have seen."

"Well now to the point of my visit at this late hour." the superintendent resumed.

"I was summoned to the Home Office this afternoon and was given instructions as to how this murder enquiry is to be conducted. You may well have guessed the circulation of these very good forgeries presents a serious problem, not only to the Royal Mint but to the national exchequer so the Bank of England are also concerned."

"And the Home Office, Sir?"

"Ah yes, the Home Office. They have their own concerns. It would appear there are elements in the Home Office who consider the proceeds from the creation and circulation of these forged coins could be being used to fund underground political activity."

"Is there any evidence for this theory?" Brannan questioned.

"I asked the same question, Inspector, and was given no proper answer. Perhaps there is no evidence, as such, merely civil servants trying to create a reputation for themselves. There has been no mention of this kind of activity in recent years at any meeting I have attended with the Assistant commissioners."

"So it is these suspicions that have involved the Home Office in what on the face of it could be either a murder for robbery or a falling out amongst thieves?"

"Not as simple as that Brannan. As I mentioned there is also the Royal Mint and the Bank of England also involved."

"But surely Superintendent, they should only be concerned with the investigation of the coining operation itself, not the murder, which could be a side issue."

"I agree Inspector and enquiries continue in the east end and further afield on the other side of the river. So far, apart from the coins you have shown me, none have been identified in this division, or if they have it was not mentioned to me this afternoon.

However, be that as it may, I received clear instructions this afternoon about this murder enquiry from the Assistant Commissioner himself.

First, your enquiries should continue in the way you suggested, but there is to be no mention of any connection with coining. Double your efforts to find where this man was living. Put one or two men, in plain clothes with that specific task. We must find where he lived and with whom he associated. That will be the key, not only to the murder but also where the coining is taking place. Pull this off, Brannan, and it would be a big feather in your cap. You could soon be a superintendent instead of acting up like last time."

"But I don't have anyone here as designated plainclothes men or with detective training."

"I didn't say they had to be designated plainclothes officers or detectives. That is the whole point and was emphasised by the Assistant Commissioner. The detective branch would not normally be involved in a Saturday night murder in Southwark so this has to be done in the normal way."

"But the normal way would not involve men in civilian clothes. My Sergeants would make the enquiries with perhaps one constable, but always in uniform."

"You are quite right. Uniform it is, but your Sergeants have other duties, so put one man on it full time with the authority to wear civilian clothes if necessary and if it is necessary to go outside the division. The A.C.C also made this clear, the enquiry needs to appear to be normal, but extra measures are permitted."

"Did the Assistant Commission give any indication what would constitute extra measures?"

The Superintendent rose "Don't try to obfuscate, Brannan. I received my orders and have passed them on to you. Now you just get on with it."

He got up abruptly and Brannan had a mental image of him gathering his skirts about him and sweeping out like a Dowager duchess.

Brannan felt no inclination to extend his day even further. What the Super wanted could wait until tomorrow and in any case his dinner was no doubt spoiling at home. His wife was a good cook but was yet to master the art of dealing with a variable meal time.

With instructions to Brewer to have some quick copies made of the drawing at the print office in the Borough High Street, he left and made his way home to Camberwell.

12

Morrison was at the front desk of the police station when Inspector Brannan arrived. Nothing much had happened since the shift change at six o'clock in the morning when all the constables going on duty were given copies of the drawing of the dead man.

Sergeant Brewer emphasised they needed to make an effort to discover if anyone on their beat had seen the man and knew if he lived locally. "But this is not the only job of the day" he barked, his moustache bristling. "This is not an excuse to go into every pub or dally with every chambermaid you come across."

George grinned to himself. Not much chance of a surplus of chambermaids in the streets of Bermondsey or the Borough. There were a few nice squares in the area with some larger houses occupied by professional folk. And a number of the medical staff of St. Thomas' and Guys

Hospitals lived in the vicinity. But young, unmarried chambermaids were still few and far between. Being single himself, George knew that only too well.

After examining the log book he went to his office, summoning Sergeant Brewer as he did so.

On his way from Camberwell this morning he considered his approach to the investigation. His instructions from the Superintendent were not as clear-cut as his superior pretended to think. Brannan decided against the suggestion of a single constable working on the case for the time being. Better to save that for when there was an identification and a clearer line what else could be discovered in the division. However, he needed to keep in mind time was running out for presenting the Coroner with an identification. There was no accounting for how this officious Coroner would react if the police went back with no knowledge of who the man was.

"Right Sergeant, you saw the Superintendent here last night. He is interested in this murder in the churchyard and has his own ideas as to how it should be investigated. You have given all the beat men a copy of the face and with some luck, during the course of the day, we could have an address. But in the meantime take one man and go to Admiral Square and make the same enquiry yourself. We know he gave that area when moving from his lodgings in Stepney and we were told that the men from the Mint made enquiries. So we will make this enquiry official from our point of view. Some of these so-called watchers do just that. Sit on their backsides and watch. We do better, we knock on doors and ask."

As usual, the sergeant responded with a military-style "Sir" and turned to leave.

The Inspector was not finished. "Take Morrison with you and when you have got the measure of the place and called at the most likely lodging houses you can leave him to finish off and come back here"

"Any reason in particular for taking Morrison, Sir?"

"Yes, he's one of the brightest here, he can be relied on to do the job thoroughly and will not slope off into a pub as soon as your back is turned."

"Very good, sir"

Brewer hesitated to make sure this was the end of the conversation this time and then left the office.

He was not convinced Morrison was a good choice. The sergeant acknowledged the constable was bright and could read and write better than most of the others, but being bright was not necessarily a good thing in a police constable when it was much more important to follow orders. People who were bright and thought for themselves did not make good beat policemen. The standing orders were quite clear on that, the main job of a police constable was to keep his beat clear of unruly or criminal elements. You do not have to be bright to do that.

But then again the main job of a police sergeant was to keep his Inspector happy so he, in turn could keep the Superintendent happy. So, Morrison it would have to be.

"Right Morrison, we are off for a little walk. Tell Smith to get out here and man the desk whilst we are away. And bring three copies of the dead man's picture."

"Where are we going Sarge," he asked as they left the police station.

"Apparently your corpse gave an address in Admiral Square. No number. So you and me are going to knock on all the doors and show the pictures and see if anyone recognises him."

"Quite a few possibilities in Admiral Square, Sergeant. And quite a few which are unlikely as well."

"Do you know Morrison I have noticed you have this bad habit of talking in riddles instead of coming out straight with what you mean. So what do you mean by the likely and unlikely?"

"Well there are several houses which are occupied by professional types from the city so I would think they are unlikely and there are a lot of the larger houses which are let off in rooms similar to where I live and I think they are probably unlikely as well. But the likely ones are those occupied by families who perhaps can't afford the rent except by taking in one or two lodgers. Our man in the morgue looked to me as being the type of person who would be a lodger. But then again, if he was known to one of the people living in one of the larger houses then he could well have been staying as a visitor rather than as a lodger. So we will still need to knock on every door."

"Well that is what we were going to do anyway, Constable, so we didn't need all that clever stuff."

George often wondered why he ever bothered to try to have an intelligent conversation with the sergeant and did so again. It was not that the sergeant was not intelligent but could rarely see further than his own nose or his most recent orders. Military sergeants were used to giving orders but for the most part, they were only repeating orders they were given by an officer. Brewer appeared to be happiest when the situation was the same at the police station. For some reason, he seemed to resist having to think or make a decision for himself.

It was to be about a ten-minute walk to Admiral Square so the sergeant needed to resume the conversation. "How come you know about Admiral Square, then, Morrison? Quite a way from your beat."

"When I left the station house to make room for the new recruits last year I didn't want to live too close to the station or to my beat. So I looked elsewhere. There were a couple of rooms being advertised in Admiral Square and went over there, but was unsuccessful."

"Why so"

"Well, my guess was for one of the houses they thought they were too posh to have a policeman living there and the others the opposite reason. Got the impression that there may have been some questionable relatives so I would not have been suitable."

13

Approaching Admiral Square they met Fred Green the local beat officer, who fortunately for him was where he should have been at that time of day. Surprise visits to beat constables were normal, the sergeant could appear at any time and on occasions even the Inspector.

The sergeant decided to include Green in the door knocking and asked if he had questioned anyone in Admiral square about the picture.

"Not so far Sergeant. Didn't know the face myself and wasn't sure if I was to do it casually or ask everyone, door to door."

Brewer didn't know either. He did not give any precise instructions regarding asking about the picture because he hadn't been given any himself by the inspector.

"You were supposed to use your common sense. Green." And left it at that.

Admiral Square was as George described. On two sides the houses were large three-storey houses with basements below and on the other two sides were old small two storey cottages. They made their way to the first of the larger houses. George took the first and went down the basement steps and knocked on the door. There was a delay until it was opened by a middle aged woman in a kind of cooks uniform.

"Yes Officer"

"Good morning, madam" George replied, ever watchful to be polite to older women, no matter their status inside the house. "Do you think you have ever seen this man, either in the house or in the vicinity?"

The woman looked carefully at the picture and shook her head. "Has never visited here as far as I know and I see everyone who comes."

"What about in the neighbourhood."

"You know little about housekeeping, young man. don't you? If you did you would know that domestics rarely see the light of day for six days out of seven so we don't see any comings and goings except for the house we live in."

The woman spoke lightly enough so George accepted the rebuff and thanked her for her time and returned up the stairway to the street level.

Sergeant Brewer had no more success at the house he had called at and neither had Green. They carried on down the street, visiting every house and getting either similar responses or no response at all.

They joined briefly together and Brewer asked Green about the houses where there had been no reply at the basement nor the front door.

"It is difficult to get to know the people in these houses, Sarge. I have only been on this beat for six months and less than half that time on days. Not all these bigger houses have servants even though you would expect them to. There are quite a few that let out rooms and most of them have daily helps. I know some of the chars, but only on nodding terms as it were. Haven't needed to question anyone in particular, so this is a rum sort of patch really."

"Rum? What do you mean?"

"Well take this house here. I have seen only two people coming and going here and yet the house has got about seven rooms, which would mean at least four bedrooms. There is no live in maid as far as I can make out. The gentleman is well dressed and sometimes walks out of the square and other times a hansom calls for him. There is no cab stands near here so he must order it. The same with the lady of the house. Gentry by most appearances, although I am no great judge of that, but this is not the west end. There is no chance in a casual way of learning anything about them. So they could be almost anybody. A remittance man come home and still spongeing off his relatives. A con man and his doxy setting up a mark, or just a managing clerk in a solicitors office with a wife who did all her own housework. Almost anything"

George was amused by this description. It was almost exactly the impression he +got from the house further down the square where he called to view a room which was advertised. The prospective landlady certainly gave herself airs and referred to her husband being "at business" all day and made no mention of any help in the house or if cleaning the room was included in the rent.

"Right we will carry on then. Green you keep a note of all the houses where we get no answer and if need be you can come back later at tea time when there should be someone at home."

Brewer went down the steps to the basement and knocked on the door. No response so after only a brief wait he climbed up to the street level and then up the two steps to the front door. In response to his over-zealous knock on the door with his staff, footsteps were heard inside. The door was opened slightly and then fully. A young woman stood there. Not very tall and dressed in the sort of clothing Brewer could not identify as ladylike or servant-like.

"Yes, officer. What did you want? And did you need to hammer on the front door like that?"

" I am sorry about that Ma'am. I wanted to be sure if anyone was at home they would hear me. I knocked on the basement door but there was no reply"

"Well, that's as maybe. But what do you want?"

Brewer was now completely out of his element and almost stammered, but recovered himself enough to say " We are enquiring about a death in the vicinity of an unknown man. Can you please tell me if you have ever seen this man hereabouts?"

The woman, still obviously put out barely glanced at the engraving. "I do not socialise here, Sergeant, so I would not know him."

"Perhaps you would be good enough to look madam, you may have passed him in the street."

"No, I am sure I have never passed him in the street and in any case he looks like any other man as far as I can tell. There must be hundreds of men who look like that. So, no I do not know him."

With that, she withdrew into the house and closed the door.

Brewer admitted to himself she had a point. There was nothing special about this face. Could have fitted a thousand men let alone the hundreds that the woman referred to. They had now been in the street for well over an hour and with nothing to show. This was not the kind of police work he was used to.

Unidentified dead bodies turned up from time to time and he had never heard of this kind of enquiry being made to find out who they were. If a relative does turn up quickly enough then he corpse is unidentified. Just that.

Brewer overtook Green who by this time had knocked on the doors of three houses a response from only one and George Morrison enjoyed similar results until the one he was at when Brewer and Green caught up with him.

14

Morrison was down at the basement door of the house which was next door to one of those he had called at when he was looking for lodgings. It was answered by a pretty young girl which made George wish he had been more successful in getting a room next door.

The girl was a little shy but took a good look at the engraved picture. "He doesn't live here" she replied to George's question, "but I am sure I have seen him. If you will wait here I will take the picture up to Madam and ask her"

"Perhaps I could come and ask her myself?"

"No" the girl quickly replied "Madam would not like that. But I will ask her,"

Morrison quickly went up the steps to the street and told Brewer what was taking place so the Sergeant decided he and Green would take a short break and go and sit in the gardens in the centre of the square until Morrison returned.

Typical, thought George, they take a break and I carry on working.

By the time he got back down the stairs to the basement door the girl returned.

"Madam says you are to come in. She will speak with you."

Now, this was an unexpected turn of events and hopefully productive.

George removed his hat and carefully and perhaps ostentatiously wiped his feet on the coir mat inside the door. He followed the maid through the kitchen then up a short staircase to the street level floor above.

Shown into a large room which faced onto the street with the windows curtained with patterned net drapes. The drapes allowed plenty of light to show the middle-aged lady seated at a desk in front of the window. There was an open notebook on the desk which she had clearly been writing in as she blotted the page before speaking.

"Please come in, Constable and sit over here and tell me about your enquiry."

George noticed the engraving was on the desk alongside her notebook.

"The image you see madam is of a man who was found dead a few days ago and we wish to identify him. He was apparently a resident in Admiral Square or nearby at some time but we do not know which house. Do you think you know him?"

"I am reasonably certain that I do constable, but of course I cannot be sure as I only met him the once."

"Where was that Madam?"

"I was visiting acquaintances at No 42 in connection with some research I was carrying out for a book. As I was about to leave, a man, I think it was this man, came into the house. For some reason, Mrs Brunswick chose to introduce us. To be honest, I have forgotten the name, which is not a very good advertisement for my skills as a writer, but there you are. She told me he was lodging there temporarily and was an engineer who frequently visited various parts of the country. I did not understand then why she chose to introduce us and made surmises in my own mind, which I will not share with you. But there you are constable. If I am wrong, then I apologise and you must come back and tell me, but I think your mystery man has lodgings at Number 42."

George was always quick to pick up on nuance in speech, "Why do you say mystery man, madam"

"Come now, Constable. Of course, he is a mystery man. You say he is dead, but you do not know who he is. A mystery."

"That's true madam." George rose and thanked the woman for her assistance and took his departure. Following the maid down to the kitchen and out and up the stairs, even though surely it would have been quicker to have let him out of the front door. But that was how the middle classes established their superiority to the lower classes by aping the mores of the upper classes and aristocracy. Before leaving he asked the maid if she knew the people at number 42. "Not very well" she replied, "just a couple, a banker or something I think.

"I may need to come and talk to you again" George said, off the top of his head. He was sure he could make up some reason for doing so. "What is your employer's name by the way?"

"Mrs Henderson"

And that was that. for the moment. With a smile at the girl, he took his leave and she waited at the open door for him to get to the top of the stairs before returning inside.

Brewer and Green were sitting quite relaxed on a bench in the little park in the centre of the square.

"Number 42, according to the lady of the house. She knew no name, only met once but she is reasonably certain."

"Right," said Brewer, as he always did, "Green you resume your patrol and me and Morrison will go directly to number forty-two.

15

Number 42 Admiral Square was similar in every way to the house where Morrison was given the address by Mrs Henderson.

Morrison was doubtful if it was a good idea for both he and the sergeant to go to the door but Brewer preceded him down the steps so there appeared to be no option but to follow.

The same procedure as before. Knocking on the door of the basement kitchen with no response. Even at this time of the day it seemed there was no activity in the kitchen. *How did the middle classes manage to go through a whole day without using the kitchen?*

So back up to the street again and rapping on the front door with the baton. It was strange, George pondered, so few of these doors held the ornate brass or cast iron door knockers which were so common in other places with similar houses. And there was no bell pulls either. *Did they not expect visitors? Perhaps they didn't want unexpected visitors?*

There was a wait of several minutes and Brewer was preparing to leave when there was the sound of bolts being drawn from inside and the door opened.

An attractive woman stood there, not young but not middle aged either. Dressed in what George surmised was the normal indoor dress for a middle-class woman, a dress but no pinafore.

Brewer spoke first as it appeared the woman was going to stand there looking at them with a questioning, but apprehensive look in her eyes.

"Good morning, madam. We are making enquiries about your lodger Mr Da Silva."

"I do not know a Mr Da Silva Sergeant".

"You do have a lodger though madam?"

"Yes, but his name is Sylvester and he is away from London at the moment."

"I see. May we come in madam, there are matters we need to discuss with you."

"Well if you must."

She stood aside as the two policemen entered and they waited in the dark hallway as she closed and re-bolted the door.

She made the way into a room somewhat similar to the one George was in previously, but the curtains of both windows in here were drawn so the room was quite dark.

The woman opened one set of curtains, but only sufficient to all the three occupants to see each other.

She did not offer them a seat and did not sit down herself.

"Now what can I do for you, Sergeant?"

Brewer produced the engraving and asked if she recognised the man.

"Well it is not a very good likeness, but I suppose it could be Mr Sylvester, but I can not be certain."

"This is the likeness of a man who has been found dead Madam and it is essential that we identify him."

"Well, it cannot be Mr Sylvester then, Sergeant. He went to Manchester or Birmingham, I am not sure which, last week. So this will not be him. If he returned to London he would have come back to his room before going elsewhere."

"Have you heard from Mr Sylvester since he went away last week?"

"No. But then I did not expect to."

"Just to be sure then Madam, what can you tell us about Mr Sylvester, how long has he been your lodger and what does he do for a living?"

"Well, he has been here a little over four weeks and paid six months rent in advance. He is an engineer of some kind, the technicalities of which are beyond my understanding and he goes away for several days at a time and then returns. He told me this would be his pattern when he first came. He does not have any meals here and did not want his room cleaned either."

"Can you tell me the last time you saw Mr Sylvester, Madam"

"I cannot be certain but it is close to two weeks ago I think. I do not get out much so the days go by and I do not notice the days of the week so much."

"What about your husband, madam? Do you know when he saw Mr Sylvester last?"

The woman paused, perhaps for the first time in the conversation, as if deciding what to respond. "I assume it would have been on the same day as myself, although my husband goes out early to his office in the city, usually much earlier than Mr Sylvester was in the habit of rising when he was here."

It was apparent to George Brewer having exhausted his repertoire of questions was about to leave the subject, so interjected:

"You said that Mr Sylvester did not have his room cleaned Madam, but presumably you have a key?"

"Yes"

"And have you been in the room since Mr Sylvester arrived?"

"What are you suggesting, constable?"

"I was not suggesting anything madam. Merely trying to establish if there might be something in the room which could help us, one way or another, to confirm if the dead man is, in fact your lodger."

"No constable. There has been no occasion to enter the room since I first showed it to him and he agreed to rent it on the terms asked."

Brewer came back into the conversation "Then perhaps you could show us the room madam in case there is something there that can help. The other alternative is for you to come with us to the mortuary to identify the corpse."

Her hand went to cover her mouth and she mumbled "I could not do that"

She sat down on the settee. Apparently recovering herself, she got up and said: "Follow me, I will show you the room."

16

The lodger's room was on the second floor in the front, looking out over the square. It stretched across the whole width of the house with two windows. The room was almost spartan having a single bed, a wardrobe a chest of drawers and a small desk with just the one chair. No easy chair, so only a bedroom.

There was nothing else to be seen. No personal effects visible anywhere, no coat hanging on the door or a carelessly left pair of shoes. The room looked and felt uninhabited.

"Did Mr Sylvester sleep here often, madam?" Morrison ventured.

"I can not really be certain. I gave him a front door key so he could come and go as he pleased. He walked very quietly but sometimes I did hear him closing the door as he left."

Brewer opened the door of the wardrobe and hanging inside was a frock coat and on the floor was a carpet bag. He took the carpet bag out and placed it on the chair.

"Does this belong to Mr Sylvester?" Brewer was becoming quite abrupt.

"I suppose it must be. I did not see him bring it, but then I do not recall him bringing any belongings with him when he came to take up the room."

Brewer opened the bag and saw there appeared to be clothing in it so moved it onto the bed and began to unpack it.

The woman became even more disturbed at this.

"Should you be doing that Sergeant? If Mr Sylvester finds you have rummaged through his personal belongings he will be extremely annoyed."

Brewer looked at Morrison so it was the constable who responded. "If Mr Sylvester is still alive, Mrs Brunswick then I am sure that as a responsible citizen he will appreciate the necessity of what we are doing. But then if he is the man in the mortuary then these items may well confirm that."

The woman did not respond and looked on as Brewer emptied the bag.

Two shirts and three collars. A pair of plain trousers. Two pairs of drawers but no under-shirts and three pairs of woollen socks.

A small leather case containing a razor, a stick of shaving soap and a brush. The kind often used by commercial travellers who were regularly away from home. Not an expensive one, no manufacturers marking, but of reasonable quality anyway.

A bit odd, thought Morrison but said nothing. He was out of his depth in this situation. Despite what he had said to Mrs Brunswick about the validity of this course of action, he was doubtful about it. So best let the Sergeant continue until something positive was found to indicate a different way forward.

There was nothing else in the bag, no spare shoes, no notebooks or documents to show what the man did for a living. The bag appeared to be no more than what it was on the surface. A bag a man would use if he travelled in the course of his occupation but not expecting to be away for more than a few days.

The lack of anything in the room to show the identity of the occupant was more than strange, it was baffling. Admitted he had only been there a few weeks and perhaps had not fully moved in because of his travelling habits. But if he was supposed to be travelling now why was his travel bag still in the room? The woman's demeanour was also odd. It was true middle-class women adopted varied attitudes in dealing with the police on the few occasions they came in contact with them: Some were overbearing looking down their noses and adopting an almost aggressive attitude, whereas others were apprehensive and defensive even when they were not being accused of any crime.

The woman seemed to have a combination of these attitudes and appeared to fear she was being implicated in some way with the death of the man. *So was she implicated?*

There was nothing more to be seen in the bag and nowhere else to look in the room. Brewer decided any further action would need to wait for the man to be positively identified as being the lodger.

"At what time are you expecting your husband home this evening Mrs Brunswick?" he asked having decided to drop any show of deference to the woman.

"I am not sure, Sergeant, usually about half-past five."

"Then perhaps, you will ask him to call at the Borough Police Office as soon as possible. He can have a look at this body to make sure if it is your Mr Sylvester."

"Yes of course."

It seemed to Morrison Brewer was about to depart leaving the bag and its contents on the bed. He thought it politic to replace the items as they were before in case this was not the man and he returned from wherever he was in the meantime.

He pulled the bag towards himself at the side of the bed to make it easier and judged it was heavier than an empty bag should be. He held the bag up and was almost certain of it. "This bag seems to have something else inside Sergeant"

"I took everything out, Morrison"

"Well I can't see anything inside either, but the weight seems to show there is something there. It is heavier than it should be."

Brewer came back to the bed and hefted the bag up for himself.

"It certainly seems heavy for an empty bag. The material is not all that thick, but the base seems more solid than usual."

Although the body of the case was the usual carpet type material the base was of well-stitched leather with a brass roundel screwed into each corner as protective feet for when the bag was placed on the ground. There was no apparent break around the edge of the base and on the inside, the floor was firmly fitted without indication of there being a compartment underneath.

Brewer was in a quandary. He was sure there was something suspicious about this bag but doubted if there was the authority to damage it in any way to discover what was hidden inside. Supposing there was nothing hidden inside and the lodger came back. Brewer hoped that Morrison was going to make some suggestions and was disturbed when the constable fished out his baton from the special pocket in his coat.

"What are doing Morrison?"

"I thought I would do some measurements sergeant."

With that, he placed the baton against the side of the bag and marked the height with his finger. Transferring the baton to the inside of the bag it was immediately clear there was a depth of more than three inches between the floor of the bag and the outside covering. Far too much to be normal.

Brewer was still cautious "I will need to take this bag back to the station to be examined Mrs Brunswick. If your Mr Sylvester returns from his travels then you can tell him what has happened. Failing that, as I said before, please ask your husband to attend at the police station as soon as convenient."

Nodding to Morrison to pick up the bag, all three left the room. On the spur of the moment, he decided on one more action before leaving the house. He was sure there was nothing in the room that would help, but perhaps the Inspector would need to see for himself. "Please lock the door, Mrs Brunswick and give me the key and any others you may have. It is essential no one goes into the room until we are certain, either of the whereabouts of Mr Sylvester or the identity of the dead man."

"Of course Sergeant. But I am afraid all the bedrooms have the same lock."

Brewer knew it would not be practical to ask for every key in the house so made do with a gruff acceptance of the situation.

"Nonetheless madam, Please lock the door, give me a key and try to ensure no one goes in until we have returned."

"Very well Sergeant. There is no one else in the house and I have no inclination to go into that room in view of what you are suggesting."

Brewer and Morrison left the house and found Green still in the square. Brewer was about to reprove him but changed his mind.

"Right Green. For the rest of the shift, I want you to keep a sharp eye hereabouts. You cant stay here all the time, but shorten your beat for today and be back in the square every half hour."

"How am going to do that Sarge?"

"For goodness sake man. Use your common-sense. You know your beat, leave out the bits that you know you can. Cut it in two. Do one half, came back here then do the other half. I shouldn't need to spell it out for you."

The sergeant and the constable then began to make their way back to the Police station.

"What do you reckon then, Sarge? Definitely seems to be a hidden compartment in here, but how are we going to get it open without cutting the bag up."

"Well just as well for you and me, we don't have to do it. That's what Inspectors are for." And for the first time since he joined the police force and came to Bermondsey, he saw the Sergeant grin. *So the old sod was human after all. I won't mention it to anyone as I'll not be believed.*

17

Inspector Brannan had mixed feelings about the report from Sergeant Brewer. It looked as though there could be an identification of the victim in time for the resumed inquest, Sylvester and Da Silva being fairly close.

But what to do about this bag? He admitted that the weight difference was fairly obvious and the depth inside the bag as once again demonstrated by Morrison with his baton was clear enough.

The problem was how could he investigate the bag without damaging the damned thing, and what if it was innocent and this Sylvester turned up.

The bag stood on his desk and he turned it over several times and could see no access to the inside of the bag from underneath. Admittedly it was a design he had not seen before and he had seen a number of them. The problem was that carpet bags were often custom made for commercial travellers, so there was no standard pattern, size or material.

This one was made of a dullish carpet material and unusually, as far as Brannan was concerned, there was a leather base with four brass rings set in the bottom. The leather was scuffed in many places so was well used, but there was nothing to show that the leather was removable. The stitching appeared to go all the way through the leather into the bottom of the carpet material so it would need to be dismantled if in fact there was a hidden compartment as Morrison suggested.

There was a linen cloth lining inside the case which also appeared to be firmly secured.

So how to attack this bag without causing more damage than could be repaired if no hidden compartment was there.

Well, there was nothing for it but to either rip out the inside lining to see what was below or try to remove the leather bottom.

"I don't suppose we have a screwdriver in the station, Brewer? do we?"

The sergeant shook his head "I don't think so, Sir, I haven't come across one and doubt if we have ever needed one."

"Right, get one of the men to go and get one, and we will see if these screws on the bottom of the bag will tell us anything for a start."

Morrison by this time was back on the desk so he was the first port of call.

"Where will we get a screwdriver, Morrison?" in an attempt to pass the job down the line as quickly as possible.

"I don't think there are any local suppliers, Sergeant. One of the marine store dealers could have a second hand one but it wouldn't necessarily be the size that you want. What size do you need?"

"The Inspector wants to try to undo the screws on the bottom of that bag to see if there is anything there."

"Well, we could probably do that with my jackknife, Sarge."

Morrison fished the knife out of his pocket and handed it to the Sergeant who returned to the office and handed it to the Inspector. "

"Morrison thinks this should do the trick, sir."

Brannan was not convinced but had little alternative but to try.

It was immediately apparent that the screws were regularly removed as they yielded to only slight twist by the point of the knife and were then easily taken out from the brass roundels which came away from the bottom of the case as soon as the screw was removed.

Nothing obvious then happened, except that a slight gap could then be seen between the top of the leather base and the side of the bag which was hidden by the thickness of the carpet.

Brannan whistled softly and decided against using any further mechanical means on the item.

"Grab hold of those handles Sergeant, whilst I see if this bottom comes away from the top."

The operation was not been completed when the office door opened and the Superintendent walked in.

"Playing tug of war gentlemen?"

Superintendent Washington appeared to have a permanent sneer in his voice. Perhaps he couldn't help it having spent too long in the military without approving of any activity that he ever came across.

"There appears to be a hidden compartment in this bag and we are attempting to discover if there is anything inside without actually damaging it."

Brannan covered his dislike of the Superintendent by either failing to use the man's name or rank or using it too frequently.

"Well carry on then. I will watch and then you can tell me what it is all about when you have discovered something."

As both Brannan and the Sergeant were on their feet, Washington went behind the desk and sat in the inspector's chair.

It did not take long to ease off the leather section from the body of the bag and it showed that there was indeed the suspected cavity. Inside there was a bundle wrapped in cloth and tied with string.

The weight of the bundle explained why the bag appeared heavier than was natural.

The string around the bundle was simply knotted and on being untied revealed that inside the cloth was a roll wrapped in greased paper. Brannan was not surprised that it was a roll of coins which would no doubt turn out to be forged. He already accepted in his mind that the dead man and the missing lodger were one and the same.

"It would appear then that you have found your forger then Brannan. Well done."

"I think, Superintendent, that we may well have found the last lodgings of the dead man and some more forgeries, but that is a long way from saying that he is the forger and we are no further forward with finding the factory."

"All that is not your problem, Inspector. Your job here in the Borough is to find a murderer, the rest is for the Mint, and for their own purposes, the Home office. If you also solve that for them, all well and good. But concentrate on the murder."

With that, he was gone.

18

So, next move? Go round to Admiral Square and search the premises before anything suspicious could be removed? Or wait for a positive identification by the husband of the landlady?

Brannan decided on the former. If the woman and her husband were involved in the coining with this Sylvester then she may well wait for her husband to come home before doing anything.

So question answered. A visit to Admiral Square it would need to be.

If he was going there himself then more than a quick look at the room would be necessary, but then a full-scale search of the house would be premature.

Just himself then and a constable. Have a look around the house and make a note of anything which would take further examination later if the proof was there. The house was unlikely to be the location of the coining factory but there could be some clues as to its location.

Despite the Super's dismissive attitude, the murder and the coining could be linked and Brannan thought that solving the murder could lead to the coining and vice versa.

Brewer was still in the room although on occasions it was easy to forget that he was, despite his size and whiskers. The sergeant rarely made a voluntary contribution and could stand silently for so long that sometimes it was possible to believe that he was asleep on this feet. And Brannan often wondered how much the sergeant took in.

Admittedly he was good at organising the station, kept the men on their toes and did not stand for any nonsense. Drunkenness on duty, a serious problem in many parts of the Metropolitan Police, was rare under Sergeant Brewer's watchful attention. There were no dismissals for this offence since Brewer arrived at the station.

But he was still a military sergeant and not a policeman. A bobby needed to be much more aware of what was going on and not rely on being told what to do.

"Sergeant, take Morrison off the roster for the rest of the week, I want him with me on this murder."

"Yes, Sir."

A smart about turn and a sergeant-major left the room whilst Brannan shook his head in despair.

There was no room to store the bag in the station safe, so he needed to be content with putting the counterfeit coins in there and the bag in a cupboard in the corner. This was used as a wardrobe for a spare overcoat in case he got caught out in the rain.

19

The Inspector was brisk. "Off we go then Morrison. I hope you know the shortest route to this Admiral Square, I have never been there before."

"It's not far Inspector. only ten minutes away. What are we going to do there?"

"I am going to interview this Mrs Brunswick, you are going to observe and make any notes that I ask you to and then we are going to look around the house and not just the lodger's room."

"There was not a lot to see in the room, sir and it is a large house for the two of us to search."

"I didn't say we were going to search. At the moment we have no evidence or reason to suppose that a crime has been committed on the premises. I will ask Mrs Brunswick for permission to look around the house to assess how this man came and went."

Seemed reasonable to Morrison so he made no further comment and they soon arrived back in Admiral Square. Fortunately for him, Constable Green was where he should have been, on the far side of the square.

"Anything happened here, Green since the Sergeant left?"

"Nothing Sir. It's always quiet in the afternoons hereabouts, not even many children in the square and most of the costers call around here in the morning. I haven't seen anyone come or go to number 42"

"Do you know this Mrs Brunswick or her husband?"

"No, sir. It's difficult to get to know anyone in this square. Although the houses are quite large, most are not fully occupied like in poorer areas, but then not many of them have domestics either. It's quite strange that way. You get the impression that many of the couples and small families have only taken short leases and intend to move on."

"No gossip about them, then?

"As I said, sir. Few domestics hereabouts so little chance to gather any information at all. During the morning when the costers are about, the maids or cooks or whatever seem to scurry out to buy and then almost run back inside again. Like I said. Its a rum area in so many ways. When people keep themselves to themselves, as it were, its hard to get a handle on them. But there is nothing to show that anything untoward is going on. No layabouts or drunks in the streets. No musicians or street singers. Not even a muffin man. I supposed they have all learned that there is no trade here and stay away."

"OK then Morrison, let's go and see if Mrs Brunswick has anything else to tell us. You carry on with your beat in the normal way now Green."

As before, Mrs Brunswick took her time to open the front door. They had not gone down to the basement as there would have been no point if there was no one in the kitchen. In any case, as Inspector of Police Brannan did not deem it necessary to adopt a tradesman's deference to the middle classes and any that did not like it was soon taken down a peg or two.

She nodded to Morrison, although he was not sure that she actually recognised him and then looked straight at Brannan. "Yes"

"I am Inspector Brannan from the Borough Police station, madam and I would like to have a few words with you."

She made no response, but stood aside and indicated that they should enter. When they were in she closed the door but on this occasion, she did not bolt it.

She then led the way into the sitting room and sat on the settee before saying "Please take a seat Inspector." which he did and Morrison, knowing his place remained standing alongside the fireplace.

"Mrs Brunswick, I am going to assume for the time being that the dead man we have at St. Thomas' is, in fact your Mr Sylvester so I will need you to tell me everything that you know about him"

"I really know very little about him, Inspector. He has lodged here for a little over four weeks, he paid a quarters rent in advance and that was that."

"Forgive me, madam. You live here with your husband and you spend the day here alone, yet you let a room to a complete stranger merely because he was able to pay a quarters rent? Did your husband check this man out to see if he was respectable? Did he give you references?"

"Please do not adopt that hectoring tone with me, Inspector. In the first place, it was my husband who brought him here so you had best talk to him about that and secondly, I am not alone in the house during the day."

"I did not intend to hector you, madam. I was merely expressing concern at the risk that you appeared to take in having an unknown man in the house when you spend so much time alone."

"Very well then, but you still need to speak to my husband and as I said I do not spend the day here alone."

"I will speak to your husband as soon as I can, perhaps when he visits the police station this evening. Who else then Madam is regularly in the house who may be able to assist us.?"

"I have a maid who comes in for the mornings and a cook in the afternoons who leaves after preparing our evening meal. Neither of them are here at the moment."

Brannan decided to make no comment at this stage as to why the maid was not in evidence when Brewer and Morrison called this morning.

"The cook is not here now?

"No, she is collecting provisions from the Borough Market."

"I will speak to her if she returns before we leave. So what if anything did Mr Sylvester tell you about his background when he came to view the room."

"He mentioned nothing of his background Inspector. My husband interviewed him in this room and whilst I was present but I do not recall much of the detail."

"Where did he live before?"

"North of the river, but he did not find that salubrious so was looking for somewhere of a better standard."

"And how long did he live at his previous lodgings?"

"I do not recall that being mentioned."

"Did he mention his occupation?"

"Some kind of engineer."

"Nothing more specific?"

"Nothing that I understood, Inspector."

"And what about before his sojourn in North London. Where did he live before that? Where did he come from?"

"That was not mentioned in my hearing."

"So what about since he has been here. Did you never discuss any of these matters with him during the course of conversation?"

"I did not have a conversation with him Inspector. You do not appear to understand that Mr Sylvester rented a room here for which he paid rent and he was entitled to his privacy. I had no reason to question him nor did I engage in any kind of social intercourse. We passed the time of day, made a comment about the weather and that was that. No conversations."

"I understand Mrs Brunswick. "Which of course he didn't. Sounded like the most unlikely of arrangements. The inspector had been a lodger himself in his early days as a police constable and was well aware that if Mrs Brunswick was telling the truth then this would be the most unusual of landladies. He left it at that and decided to see the lodgers room.

"Please be good enough to show me the room and then how Mr Sylvester came and went, whilst he was here."

The room on the second floor was as Brewer and Morrison left it so Brannan opened the drawers of the chest and the door of the wardrobe. For good measure, he looked behind both items of furniture but could not see any evidence of anything having been hidden there. The coins in the carpet bag were the only items to show that Sylvester was connected to the coining.

"Did Mr Sylvester have any visitors whilst he was here Mrs Brunswick?"

"Just the one. When he had been here about two weeks. A well-dressed man came in a hansom cab one afternoon and asked for him. I knew Mr Sylvester was in so I showed him up."

"Did he give a name?"

"No"

This was like extracting hen's teeth. Mrs Brunswick, for whatever reason had no intention of volunteering any information. If the occasion arose, Brannan would like to have her seated in front of him back at the station, where she may be more inclined to be cooperative.

"Did Mr Sylvester greet him by name?

"No"

"Did he appear to be expecting this man?"

"Yes"

"How did you decide that? Mrs Brunswick? what did he say?"

"He said 'Oh there you are, ' shook his hand and then thanked me for bringing him up and closed the door.

"How long did this man stay?"

"I do not know. I went out so did not see him leave."

"I see, thank you. Will you please show me how Mrs Sylvester came and went up to this room."

"We discussed that when he first came. I gave him a key to the front door, but I think it was after that visitor that he asked if he could use the kitchen door in the basement. I thought it odd but had no reason to refuse, so that is what he did thereafter."

"Are there stairs from the basement up to the second floor without using the main staircase."

"Yes there are, and that is what he used, so I did not always seem him come and go."

20

The cook was still absent at the market when Brannan decided that little more was to be learned at the house, so they left and he immediately rounded on the constable.

"Well Morrison, why did you and Brewer not mention that there could be others in the house who could identify this Sylvester?"

"Because Mrs Brunswick made no mention of having any domestics. There was no reply at the basement door and Mrs Brunswick herself answered our knock at the front door. She did not volunteer the information about domestic staff to Sergeant Brewer as she did not volunteer it to yourself, Sir"

"Well, the pair of you made me look a real fool being concerned about the woman being alone in the house all day when she clearly was not."

"There was nothing to indicate that she had staff, even part-time, Sir, and as I said she did not volunteer that information. If I may suggest, Sir, this reluctance to volunteer information indicates that there is something odd about the domestic arrangements of the household."

"What makes you say that, Morrison"

"The employment of domestic staff is generally considered by people of the class that live hereabouts as a measure of status. A certain level of income justifies a given number of employees and vice versa, the number of employees advertises the wealth of the employer. Most women like Mrs Brunswick, mention the staff very early on in any conversation about the domestic arrangement of the household. For whatever reason, Mrs Brunswick not only did not do that but appeared to be reluctant to bring it into the open until you pressed her on the point of being alone in the house."

"Well, now you have started speculating. What do you make of that?"

"I was not speculating sir. Merely observing what appeared to be a reluctance to be forthcoming about this lodger. I thought this morning that her reaction to the fact that he could be dead, was rather odd, but then not being married, my knowledge of female reactions is limited. It just seemed odd."

Brannan stifled a grin. "No sisters?

"No sisters, sir."

"Well, that's a pity then. It means that if your are going to learn anything about female reactions then you will need to get married. And when you have done that you will find that there are no standard reactions by a woman of any given circumstance and not even the same reaction to any two identical circumstances."

Morrison made no comment about that and wondered whether to make any others. Brannan was not consistent in his relationship with constables, even having risen through the ranks himself he rarely treated any ordinary bobby as if they were destined to do the same.

Admittedly the Borough station was not well endowed with men who were likely to end up as a Commissioner of police, but lower ranks even to Superintendent were still attainable. But those ambitions needed to be encouraged by superior officers but for some reason, Brannan appeared to be reluctant to give that.

They reached the police station and Morrison was saved from having to respond. Brannan went into his office to make a few notes of things to ask the husband supposing he turned up. If he didn't, then Morrison's impression of something odd about the household could be correct.

There was still an hour or more before the end of the day shift and Morrison was not sure if in fact he was on shift or not. If he was not on the day shift at the stations, what kind of shift was he on and how would he know when it was going to end.

The answer to his question came as soon as he asked Brewer.

"Didn't the Inspector tell you whilst you were out that you are off roster till the end of the week as you are to accompany him on this murder."

"No, he didn't mention it."

"Then you had best go and ask him what else he wants you to do."

The Inspector had not actually thought it through to that extent. The day had produced more than he expected but there were more questions than answers.

"Well we are expecting Mr Brunswick to call and identify the body. I will go with him so there is no need to overdo the police presence for that. You can stand down now Morrison and go home. Should I need you this evening I will send for you. If not be here at eight in the morning when I will have drawn up a plan to continue the enquiries."

Great. Go home but be ready to come out again so there is no knowing how long each day was going to be. At least when on the roster each day was only twelve hours long. At this rate any day could turn out to be twenty-four hours, this Inspector being very keen when any matter took his interest. It was still only five o'clock, so at least he gained an hour today, so he had better go and have a meal in case he was called out again. He could always leave a message with his landlady as to where he could be found.

21

James Brunswick presented himself at the front desk of the station and said why he was there and was taken into the Inspector's office.

"Sit down Mr Brunswick, please, I expect your wife has told you that we have a dead man who it would appear is your former lodger. This is a drawing of the dead man and your wife and another person have agreed that it appears to be a likeness of your lodger. Do you agree?"

Brunswick examined the drawing and agreed that there appeared to be a likeness.

"Before we go to the morgue what can you tell me about this Mr Sylvester?"

Brunswick paused briefly.

"Well, I do not know much about him really. We have been in our house only six months or so and it is a bit too big really. That fact came up in conversation at my office and a colleague said that he knew someone respectable who was looking for lodgings south of the river and that he could vouch for him. I arranged for Mr Sylvester to visit us one evening, he appeared to be as described, agreed to our terms including rent in advance and that was that., He moved in a few days later. In the last four weeks I have seen him no more than four times."

"You did not take up references?"

"No he was recommended by a colleague and that was good enough for me. My wife took to him so that appeared to be all that was necessary."

Brannan realised of course that as a long-serving policeman his view of the world was coloured by his employment so he did not pursue his view of the foolishness of inviting a complete stranger to live in ones home without making any enquiries as to his antecedents.

"Do you know exactly where he lived before he came to you?"

"No, I did not ask."

"And before that?"

"I don't understand."

"Where did he come from Mr Brunswick? Which part of the country or was he a Londoner?"

"Definitely not a Londoner. The Midlands perhaps, although I have never been to the north so those accents are not familiar to me."

"What about his occupation? Your wife said an engineer, do you know what kind?"

"Inspector I interviewed him in connection with the letting of a room. I did not think that an interrogation was necessary as he came recommended. As for his occupation, I know no more than my wife. Mr Sylvester said that he was a metallurgical engineer, whatever that is. I am an accountant in a bank and have no knowledge of engineering. He intimated that his occupation involved a certain amount of travelling so that he would not spend every night in the room. I know little else of him."

"Very well then Mr Brunswick, we need to establish if this man is your Mr Sylvester, so if you could accompany me to St. Thomas' hospital and have a look at him, it would be helpful. Do you have any qualms about that?"

"No I am sure I can look at a body without fainting".

The short walk to St. Thomas' and up to the morgue on the first floor was accomplished in five minutes and there was no reason for further conversation. Brannan was doubtful about what was going to be accomplished here. If Brunswick identified the man then they would not be a lot further forward. Brunswick and his wife purported to know nothing of the man although Brannan doubted that they had told all that they knew. If he fails to identify the body, they were not exactly back to square one but not far from it. Wait and see.

22

The body was wheeled out on a trolley and before uncovering the face, Brannan pointed out that the drawing and a dead face were not necessarily the same thing.

Brunswick nodded and the face covering was drawn back. Brannan watched the man's face as he viewed the copse to observe his reaction. There appeared to be very little.

"Is this Mr Sylvester?"

A pause whilst Brunswick continued to look at the dead man, as though mesmerised.

"I am not sure that it is" he eventually responded. "As I told you I only actually saw him a few times and this is a very ordinary sort of face which could belong to almost anybody."

Brannan could not argue with that. He was reluctant to draw attention to the pockmarks mentioned by his namesake as being the one unusual feature of the forging suspect.

"Did you not notice any distinguishing features about him then when you saw him at your house?"

"No. Like I said. An ordinary man, reasonably well-spoken, quite good clothes and that is all really. I think now that perhaps I could pass him in the street without recognising him as I knew him for such a short time."

Brannan realised that this was not going to be an identification that would satisfy the coroner and decided to return to the station. There was no doubt in his own mind that this was the man, if only because of the coins hidden in the secret compartment in the base of the carpet bag. He needed more, but how to get it?

If Brunswick insisted that the man was not Sylvester then it may be difficult to bring Mrs Brunswick to the mortuary. This would then only leave the man who introduced him, the maid, the cook and the woman who first pointed in this direction. One of them surely would be able to be positive, particularly the work colleague. Brannan was not sure that the evidence of the watcher would be accepted.

As they walked back to the station, Brannan broached the subject of the colleague.

"Well actually, I was not being precise there," Brunswick replied. "He was a former colleague, William Partner who no longer works for our bank. He left and went to Dublin."

"Do you think that you could obtain an address for him in Dublin. Mr Brunswick. This could be important.

"I will try when I go into the office tomorrow to see if there are any records of a forwarding address."

"And also Mr Partner's address when he was in London if you would be so good."

With that, they parted company at the entrance to the police station, Brannan having no reason to detain the man any further despite the unsatisfactory responses to many of the questions.

Brannan sat at his desk. His dinner was at home but he had promised Morrison a plan of action. Time was now pressing with only a few more days before the resumed inquest. But he could think about a plan of action at home as easily as at the station.

23

George decided to wait for an hour or so in case he was sent for and then prepared to go for a meal at his local chop house. As he was leaving, his neighbour Frank Evans also came from his room.

"Going to the chop house George? Mind if I join you?"

There was no reason for Morrison to refuse and mostly Frank was quite good company except when he was in his investigative reporter frame of mind. However, his paper came out on Thursday so there was little fear of anything which came up in conversation would hit tomorrows headlines.

The weather was fine so they sauntered round to the chophouse, as well as George was able to adapt his regulation beat form of walking. Spending a twelve hour day walking at the regulation pace of two and a half miles an hour made it difficult to adjust to walking in any other way. The normal pedestrian pace was much quicker and that of a newspaper reporter on the hunt for a story was well over three times that even if he wasn't running.

George quickened his pace to keep up with Frank and they arrived at the chop house in good time. He allowed the reporter to order the first round of drinks whilst he considered what was listed on the board as being available that evening. He decided on the meat pudding and Frank chose the roast meat.

They sipped their ale as they waited for their meals and eventually Frank broached the subject of the murder.

George had been expecting it since they left their lodgings and was still unsure how much to tell the newspaper man.

"We still don't have a name for the man. What seems to be a good lead is still waiting for an identification from someone who actually knew him. Until his identity is known then there is not much chance of finding out why he was killed and from there to who did it."

"But what about the counterfeit coins angle?"

"What counterfeit coins do you mean?"

"George for goodness sake. How many times do I have to tell you I am a reporter. I spend a lot of time around the place and in particular at the two local police courts. I attended the inquest and since that time I have seen Ex Inspector Brannan twice at your police station and then later by chance, with his son and another man at the hospital. There has to be a connection between the dead man and Mr Brannan's occupation these days."

"Well, you did not hear this from me, but Mr Brannan was of the opinion that the dead man resembled someone from the east end who he was interested in. Had no evidence against him and as far as I know, because I was not there and have not been told, the watcher who went to the hospital was not certain that it was the same man. So until he is identified no one can say if he is the man from the Stepney and therefore no confirmation that he is connected with coining."

"Does he have a name, this man from Stepney?"

George hesitated and then decided against. "I can't give you that Frank, you know that. If he is connected with coining, having you sniffing around could upset Mr Brannan's surveillance and if that happened and I was identified as your source then I would be out on my ear."

"I go along with that George. I will get it from the other side of the river."

"Well if you can do that, all well and good."

"So what is happening next?"

Their meal arrived so George was saved from having to prepare a reply to that.

It was always difficult talking to Frank. He was a good reporter and whilst working for a local paper also did stringing for some of the main papers. It was not that he could not be trusted but George was aware that the newspaper instinct was strong so would not be able to resist using information he came by, even if he thought that he was protecting his source. The fact that they lived in the same house would immediately put George under suspicion if Frank used any police sensitive information, particularly if there was unintended consequences.

It was impossible not to continue the conversation after they finished their meal. Whilst George had a predilection for detective work in fiction he was reluctant to speculate when it came to his own job.

"Look, Frank, I really don't know a great deal more than you. The Inspector says he will have more work for me to do on this case but I have no idea what it is. In fact, I am reasonably sure that he went home tonight not knowing himself how he was going to proceed. Hopefully, I will know a bit more tomorrow when I get to the station. But that is not to say that I will necessarily share it with you. Why don't you go to the station tomorrow and see what the Inspector is willing to tell you? After all, you have a vested interest here, you were there when the body was discovered and the inquest is to be resumed on Monday, so it would not be unusual for you to front up and ask if he is going to be able to name the man then."

"I had a mind to do that anyway. I only have a short list tomorrow and my editor will expect me to produce something out of nothing."

It always amused George how Frank referred to his editor when the man was actually his uncle and owned newspaper anyway.

"So how come you have been taken off ordinary duties to work with the inspector on this murder?"

"I didn't say that."

"Didn't have to. You said Brannan would have something else for you to do tomorrow which means you are not on normal duty. Don't have to be a mind-reader to work that out."

"Well yes, I am off roster for the rest of the week to work with the Inspector. That's as far as it goes for now. I don't know if I am to accompany him or to go off on my own. As I said until he comes to the station in the morning I will not know, and at the moment perhaps he does not know himself."

George was glad when the subject was dropped.

24

Friday morning saw George Morrison at the station earlier than the eight o'clock specified by the Inspector.

It was fortunate as Inspector Brannan was already there. Not exactly waiting for him but ready to tell him about the partially positive identification and to give instructions.

"Mr Brunswick says he thinks that it is the same man but refuses to be positive so I am keeping an open mind as to his reasons for that. We need something more positive than that if we are to give a name to the coroner. What I want you to do is to go back to Admiral square, see the maid and find out what time she finishes. Arrange to meet her at that time and bring her back to the station so that I can speak to her and if necessary take her to the morgue.

During the morning go to the morgue and get a copy of the autopsy report. If they cannot give you one then make one for yourself so go prepared for that.

After we have seen the maid then I may wish to repeat the process with the cook. She may well have seen the man more often if he was in the habit of going in and out through the kitchen door. But we can decide that later."

George thought that there was not much "we" involved in the planning process but then he was only a constable but he could not find much fault with the plan.

The now familiar walk to Admiral Square was made in dry weather as the rains appeared to have gone away for the time being.

Morrison was not sure if he needed to ask permission of the "lady of the house" to speak to the maid but decided that it would not be necessary if he was only making the arrangements the Inspector had instructed.

Fortunately, the young woman concerned was in the kitchen when he knocked on the door. George asked if she was aware of the possible death of the lodger and she said that she was not. Strange as this seemed, George did not pursue it leaving that to the Inspector if he deemed it significant. Discovering that she finished work at midday he arranges to return and meet her on the corner of the square to accompany her to the police station. She was only about fifteen years old and did not question these instructions. If she had been older the chances were that she would have disputed the need to go to a police station if she was not accused of anything.

George did not return to the Borough Police station but went directly to the morgue at St. Thomas' hospital. The attendant did not have a spare copy of the report and in any case, doubted if he would be allowed to part with it. However, he saw no problem with George sitting at a desk in the corner and making a copy providing pen and ink and paper for the purpose.

The report was long and medically complex using a lot of words that George never came across before. However the gist of it was that the man died from a severe head injury inflicted by a long narrow, possibly metal, instrument. A crow-bar perhaps. Death would not necessarily have been instantaneous and would not have resulted in a great external loss of blood.

George still had some time left in the morning so decided to return to the station via the watchhouse. The padlock key was still in his pocket and as there was some winter sunshine he thought that it would be a good opportunity to have another look inside.

It didn't achieve a great deal and George was not sure what he was expecting to find. He was sure that the Inspector had been back and possibly several others so the room was not going to be in the same condition as on the night when he and Frank discovered the body.

The dust on the floor was now considerably disturbed from numerous boots and even the congealed blood appeared to have been trodden on. the blood though appeared to be rather less than he remembered, but perhaps it was the lack of light on the earlier occasion which faulted the memory. All though the report did say that there would not be a great deal of blood, how much was that? He made need to ask that later. George had not seen that many bodies but remembered a man who had been kicked in the head by an angry horse. It seemed to him then that there was a lot of blood. Memory again. He may need to look into that if he was kept on the case. If there was not enough blood in the watchhouse then perhaps the murder did not happen there.

He locked up the watchhouse room again and returned to the Borough station. Inspector Brannan was in his office and Morrison reported what he had done that morning and handed over the copy of the autopsy report. He also mentioned his visit to the watchhouse and his thoughts on the quantity of blood.

"Well, we don't want to complicate this even more than it is at the moment. Until we have a positive identification of this man and can find someone that he was associating within this division then the possibility that the murder happened elsewhere is irrelevant. But it will need to be kept in mind."

George dismissed himself from the Inspector's office and went and made himself a cup of tea in the back room of the station. Then it was time for him to return to Admiral square to meet the young maid.

25

Sally Adams the maid at the Brunswick's house was already on the corner of Admiral Square when Morrison arrived.

"Come along Sally then, it wont take long to go to the station, its near the Borough Market so I suppose you have been there a few time."

"I have never been in a police station."

George grinned. "No, I meant the Borough Market."

The girl visibly relaxed at his smile so as they walked he asked her about herself and how long she had been working with Mrs Brunswick, but avoided anything which he thought the Inspector would want to deal with himself. He was still on unsure ground as far as his role in this investigation was concerned. He was well aware that this death of an unknown man was not being dealt with in the ordinary way but did not know how much he was supposed to take an initiative in talking to witnesses.

He did learn that she was fifteen as he surmised and lived with her parents a few streets away from Admiral square. She had been with the Brunswick's since they first moved in, but only worked mornings so was still looking for a full-time job. She needed that in order to properly pay her way at home. This was her first proper job since she started work, mostly occasional work, often just helping out with charring or taking in washing. She didn't want to go to work in a factory so was limited in her options but her parents preferred it this way. They thought that domestic work in a middle-class home was better than factory work for young girls.

At the station, he sat her on a chair in the vestibule and went to see if the Inspector was in. He was and was instructed to bring her straight in.

Inspector Brannan smiled at the girl and thought that Morrison should have warned him that she was so young. Still, we shall have to see what she can tell us.

"Sit down Sally. You are not in any trouble. Constable Morrison has told you that we think that the lodger at Mrs Brunswick may be dead and we need to be sure about it. So can you tell me what you know about Mr Sylvester."

"What do you want to know sir?"

"Anything you can really. First here is a drawing of a man. Do you think that it looks like Mr Sylvester?"

"Well it does sir, but it also looks a bit like Mr Brunswick."

There were so many comments about how ordinary this dead man was that Brannan hadn't even noticed the similarity with Brunswick and his only excuse was that

Brunswick was still alive and the drawing was of a dead man. He also realised only at that moment that the ordinariness of this drawing was its familiarity. The hair, moustache, sideburns and beard was of a style which became so fashionable that resulted in the similarity he was looking at now. Many of them were fashioned on the style adopted by Prince Albert Edward the eldest son of Queen Victoria.

"So this could be Mr Sylvester then Sally?"

"Yes, I suppose so."

"So what was he like to talk to then Sally, was there anything different about him."

"Talked a bit funny really, but I don't know where he was from. Not from Devon or anything like that as my friend's granddad came from Devon so I know how they talk down there."

"Ever been to Devon?"

She laughed out loud then. "Lord no, never bin anywhere but the Borough. Went to see the Lord Mayor's show once though."

"So what about his face then, apart from the beard and so on. Anything special about that? Did he smile when he was talking or was he serious all the time?"

"Didn't talk to him much. I asked him once if he wanted his room cleaned but he said no and I didn't ask again."

"The face?"

"Didn't look at his face, sir."

Brannan shook his head. He knew exactly what she meant. Taught from an early age that to get on in domestic service you had to know your place. And knowing your place meant keeping the head bent when being spoken to and only answering direct questions. This girl was not going to be any help as a witness so she might as well go home.

He told Morrison to show her out and to then come back.

"Right Morrison if the cook is not going to be any more help than that girl then there is not much point in bringing her in. We are not going to be able to prise her away from her kitchen this afternoon anyway without causing a rumpus. Brunswick is supposed to get home from work about five o'clock and no doubt they eat their supper or dinner or whatever they call it soon after. I get the impression that this accountant is not as well paid as all that which will be the reason for the part-time staff so he may well eat his main meal in town. Anyway, I need to keep the pressure on him about the antecedents of this Sylvester. The story is a bit too convenient for keeping secrets. Introduced reliably by a work acquaintance who has gone to Ireland so he cannot answer for what he knows.

I am going to continue on the basis that Sylvester and Da Silva are one and the same. You go back to Admiral Square, knock on the doors that we got no reply from before, speak again to your original informant and then wait until Brunswick arrives home and ask what he has discovered at his office. You can also speak to the cook before you leave."

"Did you read the autopsy report, sir?"

"Yes, I did. Why do you ask?"

"I didn't understand all of it sir but have wondered about the amount of blood. Perhaps we should ask the doctor to speculate about that in case it indicates that perhaps the murder did not take place at the watchhouse, but somewhere else."

"Well you saw the body before I did, Morrison. Was it moved before I arrived?"

"Not significantly sir"

"Well it seemed to me that the blood was under the head which seemed to show that it ran out from the wound soon after it happened, surely?"

"I agree sir, but wonder if that is what we were supposed to think. What if the murder took place somewhere else and the blood was placed there in exactly the right place?"

Brannan almost exploded. "For crying out loud Morrison don't try to introduce more mystery than we already have already. This is not a detective story, this is straightforward police work and we need to deal with what we have not what we think might have been."

Morrison thought better of trying to respond to this. Yes, it was police work and not fiction but the facts did not add up, no matter what the inspector thought so there was a need for speculation. Still he had to do as he was told, so left it at that.

"The cook sir. How shall I know if she will be any more reliable than the maid? We still do not have a positive identification. What about Mrs Brunswick? Would she be any more reliable?"

"I agree we do not have a positive identification and it would be better if we did. If the cook mentions anything which you think would be useful and if she is mature enough to handle seeing a dead body then arrange for her to come in tomorrow morning and we will take her to the morgue. As for Mrs Brunswick, I am saving her for later. I am not happy with her responses and that room was much too bare for a man who lived there for over a month and has only gone away for a few days. If as she said he had gone on a trip then why was the bag still there and why was she not surprised to see it? She claimed that she had not seen it before but that seems unlikely. And no conversations between a landlady and a lodger in four weeks. I don't believe it. But we need something more to put the pressure on her. So an identification would give us reason for compelling her to attend the station, and sitting here would give her a different perspective on her situation."

"Very well sir. Do you think you will still be here when I return."

"Of course I will Morrison. I work as hard as any constable here you know, despite what some of the lazy buggers think. Get off down to Admiral square and let me know when you get back and don't slope off to the chop house in between. You are still on duty and not on holiday despite not pounding the beat. As I said before this is police work and needs to be done in a proper fashion."

Morrison took this as dismissal and left the office whilst Brannan began to think again about what they learned today.

26

It was well gone three in the afternoon by the time Morrison got back to Admiral square. He decided that Mrs Henderson would be his first port of call if only to see the pretty Alice again. She answered the door of the basement and seemed pleased to see him again.

"Have you come to see me constable?" with a twinkle in her eye.

"I have indeed Alice, but officially I am here to see Mrs Henderson unfortunately so I am not allowed to dally with you even if that is what I would prefer."

"You had better come in then Constable Morrison of the Borough Police Station and I will let the lady know that you have come to see her especially and ask if she wishes to see you."

With that, she closed the door behind him and was gone through the door which led up to the floor above.

She was not gone long.

"Come with me if you please Constable George."

She turned and led the way with George Morrison admiring the rear view and having difficulty in not touching. Despite being single and twenty-four years old, he had little experience of flirtatious encounters with young women. He had no sisters to advise him and he enjoyed little of what would be called a social life before joining the police and none since. The thought crossed his mind that he would need to get some tips from Frank Evans who he was sure was more experienced in these matters.

Mrs Henderson was seated at her desk as she was on the previous occasion but did not get up when George arrived., Presumably she had been writing but her notebook was closed.

"Good afternoon Constable. Please sit down and Alice can bring us some tea whilst you tell me the reason for your visit."

"That is very kind of you Madam, but tea will not be necessary."

"May not be for you, but it is for me and I prefer to drink my afternoon cup of tea in company. It is time for my tea and fortuitously you are now my company."

George seated himself as bid but Mrs Henderson remained at her desk but turned towards him.

"Now then Constable. The reason for your visit."

Morrison explained that it appeared that the man at the morgue was indeed the lodger at number forty-two but there was no positive identification.

"Well I did notice that not only was it an ordinary enough face but as a writer, I have thought that this Prince Albert face hair on so many male faces today whilst being fashionable could almost be a disguise. I have even been thinking about using it in one of my books if ever I get round to writing a detective story."

George was not sure if she was having some amusement at his expense but decided against it.

"I realise that you only met the man the once, Madam, but the hair apart, was there anything on the face or the man's build that you thought might be sufficiently significant?"

Alice returned to the room with a silver tray holding teapot, cups and a plate of biscuits which she placed on a small table close to the chair on which George was seated.

"Shall I pour madam?

"Yes please, Alice. The constable can help himself to milk and sugar if he wishes."

After dealing with this domestic arrangement the maid left the room and George waited to see if the woman would resume the conversation whilst drinking her tea or wait.

She picked up her cup, drank a few sips and then replied to his question.

"Starting at the top as it were, the hair was reasonably well groomed, beginning to thin in places but no grey that I noticed. The skin was a little florid by nothing that indicated a heavy drinker. Eyes quite sharp and an assessing kind of gaze and ears which did not protrude beyond the side whiskers. His stance was upright without being military but I did not see him walk except for a short distance so I could not assess his gait. He did not carry a cane."

The pause here gave Morrison to the chance to ask, before he forgot, "A hat, Madam. Did he wear a hat?"

"Yes, of course, he was wearing a hat. Few, if any gentlemen go abroad without a hat."

Punctured again but George was not abashed, took another sip of his tea, he had not touched the biscuits no matter how inviting they looked. "Do you recall the type of hat?"

"Yes, a fairly standard bowler hat of the type that, apart from the signs of wear is almost indistinguishable no matter it being worn by a costermonger or a city accountant."

"Were there signs of wear madam?"

Mrs Henderson almost sighed. "You expect too much, Constable, from a brief few moments, virtually on the doorstep. No, I did not observe whether the hat was well worn or brand new. There is a well-known hatter in the square and for all I know he could have bought it there five minutes previously."

"What about Mrs Brunswick, Madam? You said that you knew her in connection with some research you were doing for a book?"

"What about her, Constable? The man may have been a lodger of Mr and Mrs Brunswick but that does not give you the right to pry into her private life or my relationship with her."

George was not sure if he should try to mollify this attitude or to plough on.

"It was not my intention to pry into matters which are private or personal, Mrs Henderson, but I am sure that you realise that in a matter of murder it is difficult to know when information is personal and when it could be germain to identifying the culprit."

"I accept that constable and I am well aware of my public duty, but my conversations with Mrs Brunswick were on a completely different subject and will not be relevant to your enquiry. You may accept my word on that."

George realised that he had chosen the wrong time to enquire about the relationship between his hostess and Mrs Brunswick and perhaps now was the time to admit defeat in that area.

"Of course Madam. I am grateful for the assistance you have given me so far and I am sure it will be of use in our subsequent investigation and hopefully result in us identifying the killer"

He rose to leave but was waved down again by the woman.

"It was not my intention to be sharp with you constable. A writer needs to gather material where she may and sometimes it is necessary to disguise and protect the source of that material. I will think about what you have said and consider if there is anything in my discussions with Mrs Brunswick that would further assist with your enquiries. If there is then I will certainly communicate them to you. Now before you leave, are you certain that the body is that of the man from number forty-two or would it assist if I came and saw the body?"

George had difficulty in disguising his surprise at this turn of events and realised that he would need to react quickly

"Whilst it was not our intention to ask you to do that, Madam, it cannot but be helpful. When do you think it would be convenient?"

"Well now, of course. As it happens I have ordered a hansom for four o'clock to go somewhere else. This seems to me to be much more important, so when it arrives, you and I will go together to St. Thomas'. You may remain here for the ten minutes or so whilst I ready myself and then we will be off."

The animation of all this was another surprise for George. Alice returned to the room to clear the tea things and George took the opportunity of having one of the biscuits. He told the maid of her employer's decision and when she left the room he decided to remain standing and if there was time to have a look at the notebook on the desk. It was not to be as Mrs Henderson returned to the room dressed for the street. The sounds of the hansom cab in the street indicated that they would be able to leave immediately.

27

Mrs Henderson was full of surprises as far as George Morrison was concerned. Her demeanour in the morgue was brisk and matter of fact. The atmosphere of the place which affected George almost went unnoticed by the woman.

The body was produced, she looked at it closely and before either the attendant or George could prevent it she turned the head with her gloved hand so that she could see the face at a different angle.

"I am certain that this is the man I saw at Mrs Brunswick's house a few weeks ago."

She then turned on her heel and left the room with George scurrying along behind her. Along the corridor, down the stairs and through the courtyard to where the hansom cab waited for her return. George realised then that his feeling that this woman was old and somewhat infirm was completely wrong.

She got into the cab and then turned to the constable. "If after considering what I should do further in this matter, I decide to take you into my confidence regarding my discussions with Mrs Brunswick I will send Alice with a message for you to come and see me again."

"I shall look forward to that, Madam."

"I am sure you will, Constable."

With that, the driver, who had been listening, took it to be a signal and whipped up the horse and they were gone down St. Thomas Street towards the Borough High Street. George followed on foot and took his own amusement at catching them up at the junction where they were stuck in a traffic jam and he surmised that he would be back at the station before they moved again. It was not part of the police constable's duty to organise traffic even if he was on the beat.

28

Having gone beyond his original instructions from Inspector Brannan it would be best to try to report back at this stage and see in there was any change in the decision to bring Mr Brunswick back to the station.

Brannan listened to George's recount of his meeting with Mrs Henderson, her positive identification of the body and her offer to possibly disclose more about her previous discussions with Mrs Brunswick.

The inhabitants of Admiral Square seemed to think that they could deal with the police in any manner that they chose. This was a murder enquiry and as citizens, they were duty bound to supply whatever information they held to the police. Not pick and choose for themselves. If necessary he would have both of these hoighty toighty women in for questioning at the station and they would soon learn where their duty lay.

"And there is the confirmation of the hat" Morrison added almost as an afterthought.

"Sometimes you lose me in your thought processes, Constable. Why is the hat significant at this stage?"

"Only as an added confirmation of the identity, Sir and the fact that it was not at the place where the body was found. I have been thinking that this is almost confirmation that the murder did not take place there. If the murder took place elsewhere and the body taken to the watchhouse with the intention of making it appear that this was the site of the crime, they may not have realised that the absence of the hat would be significant."

"I see what you mean, Morrison. However, we do not have the hat and we do not have the murder weapon either for that matter. The area has been searched thoroughly and neither found."

"Which perhaps adds to the possibility that this was not the murder scene at all." George threw in and then decided that perhaps that was sufficient initiative from a constable who was only supposed to be doing the legwork in this enquiry, not thinking about it.

The Inspector was thinking along the same lines but did not say so. Admittedly he had pushed the possibility that the constable was talking about to the back of his mind. Now it was necessary to give it much more serious consideration as this would change the scope of the enquiry. But then perhaps not. If the Brunswicks were involved then the murder could well have taken place at the lodgings although there was no indication of that in the man's room. But a full-scale search of the house would require a warrant and he doubted that there was sufficient evidence at this stage to convince the superintendent to apply for one from the local magistrate. The problem was that if the murder was committed in the house in Admiral Square then the more time that elapsed before a search would mean that the place would be as clean as a whistle before it could take place. Then they would be left further back with the enquiry than before.

Perhaps another strategy may be necessary. If the Brunswicks were involved than it could be better to leave them unaware that they were suspect and to pursue all the other enquiries and to leave them thinking that they were in the clear.

"Right then Morrison, I still do not want to leave Mr Brunswick thinking that his lodger's referee is not important but not admitting that we have confirmed the identity. So go and see him early this evening to see if he has an address for this man Partner, where he is now or at least where he used to live. Leave it at that, no commitment on the identification only that we need some more confirmation. You may ask if he got the impression that Partner and Sylvester were friends or mere acquaintances. If he comes up with some addresses then all well and good, if he doesn't, tell him that we will need to go to the Bank ourselves in the morning to get the information. That should clarify his mind that this is important. We only have until Monday for the inquest, but he will not know that is not so important at this stage."

Another implied dismissal so George returned to the station office and realised that there would not even be time for a cup of tea before making his way to Admiral Square. Oh well he will do it the other way round. Admiral Square first and then a cup of tea on his way back.

29

The inspector had said not to bother with the cook, but George thought that a few words would not come amiss so went to the kitchen door.

A girl child answered his knock but a cook looking person came to the door.

"Good evening madam. I have come to see Mr Brunswick, do you know if he is at home yet?"

"Yes, he came home about ten minutes since but they are not ready for their supper yet and it is not ready for them either so I can't stand here talking to you."

"I don't want to get you into any trouble, cook. So what do you think, shall you let them know I am here or shall I go and knock on the front door."

"No need for that. I will tell them you are here in a few minutes when I have finished what I am doing."

George took that as an invitation to come in. The food smelled delicious and he assumed that the cook would be able to work and talk at the same time.

"Did you know the lodger, Mr Sylvester?" he asked.

"Knew he was here but never saw him."

So that was the end of that possibility, but at least it was out of the way.

"I thought he had a key to this door here and came and went through the kitchen."

"So well he might have done, but not whilst I was here so it must have been before I arrived in the afternoon and after I left at night."

Wiping her hands on her apron and brushing herself down "I'll go and let the master know you are here and see if he wants to see you."

The little mite who had opened the door was almost hiding in the corner. A scrap of a thing about nine or ten years old who was obviously the scullery maid. "What is your name" he said. She didn't know if she was supposed to reply or not but eventually she bobbed her knees and said "Minnie, Sir."

"Do you work here Minnie?"

"Yes sir, cook is my aunt."

This little girl was much too diffident for a Bermondsey child. Most of the virtual street arabs that Morrison saw, even the ones from respectable working families were much more alert that this little titch.

It was not unusual for children of this age to be working in domestic service and the chances were that she was not actually employed by the Brunswicks but by the cook herself.

The domestic arrangements of the so-called middle classes were complicated by the various layers of this class of people. Sitting as they were between the aristocracy and the labouring classes there were several stratas of them depending on their wealth or income. Tradesmen and shopkeepers were often described as "middling" and those employed in the upper levels of banking and larger commercial enterprises thought of themselves as being a bit above that.

The number of employees in the household was often an indication of the status of the family, the more their income, the more staff they could afford, and flaunt when the occasion arose.

The cook returned and handed Morrison a piece of paper on which was written two addresses, one in Dublin the other in Stepney. "The master says that this is the information that you need and he is too busy to see you now."

There was no option but to accept this so taking his leave he made his way back to the station. The Inspector may be annoyed that he had not had the opportunity to speak to Brunswick but there was no way in which he could have insisted.

30

It was not unusual for the Superintendent to arrive unannounced at the Borough Police Station. He was based at the brand new specially built station in Bermondsey Street where he occupied a large office with a large desk that he could lord it in. When he first moved into the new office he was in the habit of sending for the Inspectors based at the Borough to come to see him.

That had gradually changed and he soon reverted to his old habit of calling in without notice and had even been known to visit a constable on his beat. But he soon tired of that exercise of authority.

Now he felt the weight of the administrative duties which the police service was gradually imposing on all its underlings. The Commissioner, Sir Richard Mayne was constantly issuing instructions through the two assistant commissioners and sometimes directly on a multitude of subjects. On one occasion he had sent an order making constables responsible for the prevention of snowballs being thrown in the street. And Commissioner Mayne required reports that all instructions were being followed.

But this was not the reason for his visit today. As always though he began with a question rather than starting with why he was there.

Brannan was used to this but it irked him every time.

"So what progress on this murder of the coiner, then Brannan."

"We have a positive identification that he is the man who was lodging in Admiral Square and I am hopeful that a previous address in the east end will get an identification from there which should confirm that this is the man that the Mint team were watching, albeit unsuccessfully."

"But why was he murdered, man?"

"That we do not know. We have been held up with the lack of identification so now we can try to confirm his various movements whilst he has been in the division. There is still no information as yet that will pinpoint a motive for the murder. It could still be a street robbery and have nothing to do with the man's personal life or of his activities with the coining operation."

"These coins are still surfacing so his death has not stopped that." The superintendent rejoined, "And the Home Office has been on to me again as well as a letter from the Commissioner. They want some results, Brannan, and I need to be able to tell them something. Have you put a man specifically on this case?"

"Yes, sir. I have followed your instructions on that and you may recall that the instructions from the assistant commissioner was that this was to be handled as a routine murder enquiry, so this is what I have done. I have interviewed witnesses myself and the body has been viewed for identification. All this is normal but takes time."

"So what is your next move? Its a week now since the man was found."

Brannan allowed his impatience show, "I might point sir that it is only a week. Our next move is as I indicated. I am expecting the address of the man who recommended the lodger to become known today or tomorrow. I will then send my constable in civilian clothes, as it will be outside the division, to that address and also to the previous lodgings of the dead man. If you think that it would expedite matters we could ask H or K divisions to make these enquiries, but that would change the normal pattern of an enquiry."

"No, no there is no need to extend the murder investigation beyond this division. That has been made quite clear, otherwise, we could have had an inspector or at least a sergeant from the detective branch here several days ago. No, carry on as you have suggested. I can send a report to the Commissioner today telling him what you have told me. He will receive it tomorrow and if he does not agree then he will soon let us know."

Brannan mollified pursued the Home Office angle. "What about the civil service then, Superintendent? Have they come up with any further information about their interest in the matter apart from the sophisticated coining?"

"No they have not told me anything direct and I have not been invited to any further meetings on the subject. There are the stories in the press regarding the Fenians both in Ireland and America, despite the civil war and there are always murmurs about Russian spies being ignored over here. Both Russian and Irish revolutionaries are always in need of money either to further the cause or to buy arms. They would be obvious suspects if there really is large-scale forging going on."

"Do you doubt that it is large scale?"

"I know no more than I have been told by the Mint. They say that there are a lot of coins, identical to the ones that you found which indicates to them that the operation is almost industrial. Of course, they have no means of knowing how many are actually in circulation. these coins pass muster in most circumstances and in the ordinary course of events most coins just go round and round and never go near a bank or any other place where they would be subject to scrutiny. But as for large-scale, why half- crowns? If I could make coins this good I would make them of a larger denomination, so I am not convinced that this is a big operation."

"You are right to be sceptical, Sir, but then if it is a big operation and there are thousands of pounds worth out there then the Mint and indeed the Treasury are right to be concerned."

The Superintendent sighed and got to his feet. "Well let us hope that this murder is just that and you can bring in a culprit, then the forging will not be our problem."

Brannan was surprised by this attitude and said goodbye to the back of his superiors head as he went through the office door.

31

The Inspector looked at the piece of paper Morrison brought from Brunswick.

"Make a note of these addresses in your notebook Morrison and also number 39 Princes Square. First go to Princes Square in the morning and the other east end address after. Speak to these landladies and find out if Da Silva or Sylvester or he may even have used a different name at his lodgings left anything behind and in fact everything that she remembers about him. The room will have been relet but get a look at it anyway to compare it with the one in |Admiral Square.

Then go to the other address and find out all you can about this chap Partner. Take one of the drawings with you and see if Sylvester ever visited there."

Morrison was not familiar with the east end of London. He was born in Kent and made very few forays to the other side of the river Thames. As a policeman, there was little spare time so since he came to the Borough police station he spent most of his time in Southwark, working and sleeping. A few years earlier he had been sent over to the City and then to Bethnal Green on an enquiry but had not been back that way since.

He voiced his lack of knowledge of the east end and got short shrift in response.

"It's not darkest Africa for crying out loud Morrison. Its only on the other side of London Bridge and most people over there speak English the same as you and me, so go over the bridge and ask one of the City bobbies for directions. You will be in civilian clothes yourself so there should not be a problem.. I hope you have some clothes which will not draw attention to yourself."

The instruction about the civilian clothes came as a surprise so George could not stop himself expressing it.

The Inspector was now becoming impatient and began to wonder if he had made the right choice in Morrison for this enquiry.

"Sit down man and I will go over it all for you. I can't come with you tomorrow to hold your hand nor can I spare a sergeant to do that either."

George accepted the put down even though it was completely unnecessary and unfair. He had been in the police long enough to know that the wearing of uniform at all times was mandatory except in exceptional circumstances. Another mandatory instruction was that even Inspectors were not permitted to make an arrest or even enquiries outside their own division.

"You know that the finding of these counterfeit coins alters the complexion of this enquiry. You know that the Mint is involved and I will tell you that the Superintendent has been passed specific instructions about the conduct of this enquiry from the Commissioner. One of those instructions is that the enquiry needs to be low key and for that reason, plain clothes are required as well as enquiries outside the division. There will be no repercussions on yourself if you are challenged by anyone from another division. So get on with the job tomorrow. It should not take too long. I will be here when you get back and dependant on what you discover I will decide what our next move is going to be."

Somewhat mollified Morrison left the room and realised that perhaps he protested his ignorance too much. Oh well, at least he had nothing else to do that day and could have the evening off. He wondered if the instruction about wearing plain clothes started now and he could invite Frank this time to a trip to the West End. He was not sure about the one suit that he owned being unobtrusive as required but it would have to do.

32

Frank Evans was leaving his room as George arrived back at the lodgings so the constable made his suggestion about an evening out.

"Well now, George, as you can see I am on my way out as I have arranged to take a young lady to the music hall. You are very welcome to join us if you wish, I will be back here within the hour with the lass in tow, so plenty of time to get yourself togged up in your glad rags"

"I would not like to be a gooseberry, Frank."

"Gooseberry you would not be, young feller me lad, this is my sister who is visiting my uncle in Camberwell and I have promised to show her the sights. For this evening that includes a music hall in Stepney. I have not been there myself so am a bit apprehensive about Susan's reaction, but I have heard it is a very new and well-conducted place. So if it is not any good you can help to take the edge of her disappointment and we can go on somewhere else."

There was only a moment or two to accept or decline the offer. In view of his earlier proposal that they should go out together it would have appeared churlish for him to refuse, so accept he did

"I am not sure about glad rags Frank, I only have the one suit."

"We are the same size, I have several, go in and choose one of those and I will be back with Susan and we can ask her opinion as to whether you pass muster."

Then he was down the stairs and off

George inspected Frank's wardrobe and considered that most of the jackets were of a style that he thought would not suit him. Brighter colours and checks that he thought would draw attention to himself in a way that he knew that he would dislike.

So it was back to his own one and only suit, dark jacket and waistcoat and trousers that he knew fitted well. A white shirt and black tie made it sufficient to be reasonably well dressed without being showy.

The journey to Stepney was not long in the cab that Frank returned in with his sister. Susan refused to make any comment on George's attire claiming that she had insufficient knowledge of mens' clothing. She turned out to be a very pretty young woman, a little younger than her brother and quite outgoing.

Wiltons Music Hall Was not what Frank expected even though he had never attended one. He anticipated something like one of the theatres he had attended, situated on a main road, whereas Wiltons was in a side street which was actually named Graces Alley. The exterior, however was like a theatre with several lamps lighting a brightly painted facade decorated with playbills. The inside was almost opulent in sharp contrast to the streets around which were grey and miserable, not dissimilar to the Borough.

The various acts were introduced by a chairman who used as many long words as he could fit into one sentence. George being well read was sure that many of them were invented words so quickly became irritated with this manner of introduction. Perhaps music hall was not going to be his preferred form of entertainment.

Susan appeared to be quite enamoured of all the proceedings even though some of the songs were quite bawdy. She either did not recognise a double entendre in a song or just ignored them. George became a little bored when the second set of gymnasts appeared. One set of low wire trapeze artistes was quite sufficient for him so he made an excuse to leave his seat and wandered out into the foyer.

It was decorated as usual with copies of old posters and drawings of famous artistes who had appeared there in the past. Not being a follower of the music hall, most were unknown to George there was a small stall in one corner with printed programmes and copies of cartes de visite of famous persons. George browsed the cards, passing over those of the Queen and members of the royal family and looked at those of good-looking women in theatrical poses. He noticed one whose face appeared to be familiar, although the cards themselves were small only a little over two inches by three inches, and the portraits, for the most part, were full length so the face was not that easy to distinguish one from another. The name on the card was Lily Laverne.

The stall was attended by an elderly man so George asked if he knew anything about this Lily Laverne.

"Yes she appeared here for a season shortly after we opened but she was a little too young for the hurly-burly of music hall and in any case wanted to be an actress. I believe she got a small part in one of the licensed theatres but haven't heard of her since so suppose nothing much came of it."

George wondered why such a brief appearance at Wiltons justified the production of a carte and voiced this to the man.

"Simple really" he responded with a smile at the young man's naivete, "When Mr Wilton reopened this place after the rebuilding he spent a lot of money on advertising, including having the cards made of almost everyone who performed here, good, bad or useless. At first, the cards sold quite well towards the end of a performance but then only of the stars as it were and eventually interest dwindled away. So we still have all these here and you can have anyone you like for sixpence."

George thought that sixpence was a lot of money to spend on a vague idea of recognition and decided to return to his seat.

Remembering his task for the next day he decided to ask the old chap about the addresses he would need to go to.

"Wellclose square and Princes square? Well, you won't have far to go from here. Wellclose is just up the alley and Princes is along the 'ighway."

Pleased with that piece of police work he resumed his seat alongside Susan Evans and gained the impression that by this time the novelty was wearing off and she was not particularly enjoying her evening out.

George was as pleased as she was when Frank announced it was the time he had arranged for the cab to collect them. They returned to Bermondsey and after George left them at the lodgings Frank continued on his way with his sister.

Although the evening was quite enjoyable George regretted that he had not had more time to engage Susan in conversation. He doubted if there was going to be another opportunity so that was a relationship with no chance of flowering into anything more.

Returning to his room, his mind went back to the card of Lily Laverne at Wiltons music hall, but he still struggled with identifying the real-life face that the photograph had brought to mind. No matter, if it was important it would come back to him, perhaps when he was less tired.

33

Saturday morning and George was unsure how to proceed. His instructions were to visit the two addresses in Stepney and fortunately he now knew where they were so that saved a little bit of hassle. But the instructions were direct from the inspector but George was not sure if was to report in to the station before going off to the east end. This was all new. He had never heard of any other constable being sent in civilian clothes to another division to make enquiries.

However, he did not want to go to the station in his own clothes and draw attention to himself when it was clear that the method of this enquiry was so different from normal. He didn't want the bother either of dressing in his uniform, reporting to the sergeant and advising him of his movements and then returning to his lodgings and changing into his own clothes again. It was clearly a matter of damned if he did and damned if he didn't.

Georges natural inclination was always to be on the safe side. Whilst he was not uncomfortable as a policeman many of the regulations and semi-military attitudes irked him and he often thought that he should consider another profession. His uncle, who was an inspector in the Kent police, had warned him about this. Whilst he was supportive of George's decision to join the London police he considered that perhaps the life of a constable would not be to his liking. He could be ambitious but promotion in all police forces was slow and most constables did not rise to be sergeants let alone get any higher. It took his uncle twenty years to rise through the ranks to be an inspector.

On this occasion, though George decided to accept that it would be reasonably expected of him to proceed first thing on the job given to him by the inspector without reporting to a sergeant. Hopefully, Inspector Brannan has apprised the sergeant of his instructions.

From his observations the previous evening he knew that the journey was in in the region of a mile's walk which should not take him more than half an hour using double the regulation pace of two and a half miles per hour as a yardstick.

The weather was dry, if not fine, so it would not be an unpleasant walk and if he followed the route taken by the cab it should be straightforward provided there were not too many new things to see on the way to divert his attention.

It was a short walk to London Bridge. As he crossed, he was glad that his new overcoat was a warm one as the wind was blowing up the river and was as cold as when it left the estuary. On the other side of the river and down past the Billingsgate fish market busy still at this time in the morning. Going around the back of the Tower of London his route took him along Royal Mint Street which until recently was called Rosemary Lane. He noticed the Royal Mint refinery as he went along the street and was aware that it was a private company and not part of the Royal Mint. He wondered how many of the workers in there would have the skills to engage in processing metals to make counterfeit coins.

Eventually Royal Mint Street became Cable Street and then turning into Well Street almost immediately there was Graces Alley, past Wiltons Music Hall into Wellclose Square.

George was surprised to find that this was not a slum area as he anticipated. Not unlike Admiral Square although most of the houses were considerably older with one or two timber faced houses. Sitting in the centre of the square was a church surrounded by gardens and railings.

Much as he would like to have seen more of this strange arrangement there was a job to do and made his way to Princes square following the instructions of the old man at the music hall the previous evening.

More surprises here. There was a church in the middle of Princes Square also. This square contained similar buildings presumably from the same period of construction as the other, but this area, even though only a short distance away was clearly more run down.

Number 39 was a three-storey structure, and there were litter and broken brickbats on the pavement but the stairs up to the front door were clean. George noticed that the doorstep was blackleaded – a good sign for lodgings. There was an iron door knocker which George used with gusto.

The door was opened by a child not dissimilar to the one in the kitchen in Admiral Square not quite as clean perhaps, but presentable enough George knew no name for the landlady here so simply asked, "Is the landlady at home."

"Aint no rooms to let ere." was the unsmiling response

"I am not looking for a room. I am a policeman and I wish to speak to the landlady."

"Don't look like no copper to me."

Before George could engage in any further disputation with this unsmiling, antisocial urchin a woman appeared in the doorway behind the child and gently ushered her behind.

Turning then to the policeman she asked: "What is it you want then?"

"Good morning madam. I am a police officer from the Borough High Street, hence the reason for being out of uniform, as the child noticed. I am making enquiries about a former lodger of yours who has been found dead in Southwark."

"Which lodger is that then?"

"A Mr Da Silva or he may have called himself Sylvester"

"Never been anyone of that name here."

She began to close the door. The constable hastily put his foot on the doorstep and produced the picture of the dead man from his pocket. "Perhaps you will be good enough to look at this picture and tell me if you recognise the man."

George considered that this woman was quite capable of shutting his foot in the door, however, she took the engraving and looked at it. "He said his name was Shaffer and was here a couple of months and left about six weeks ago"

Guessing that she would not wish to draw too much attention from her neighbours by remaining on the doorstep for two long he asked.

"May I come in madam, as I need you tell me as much as you can about this man."

With a toss of her head, she opened the door wider and shepherding the child in front of her lead the way into a small front room, leaving George to close the door behind him.

"Sit yourself down and tell me what this is all about."

"As I said madam, what is your name, by the way? The man was found dead in Southwark a week ago."

"I am Sarah Jones, I rent this house and take in lodgers. If they pay their rent and give me no trouble then I am not nosey about their business or where they came from, so I cant tell you anything about Shaffer."

"Perhaps then a few questions. Did he have a rather unusual carpet bag and did he tell you anything at all about his employment?"

"Yes he owned a bag and he mentioned when he first came that he would not always be here because he travelled up North from time to time but would keep the room on whilst he was away."

"Did he have a room to himself and how often did he go away whilst he rented the room."

"Yes he had the room to himself and I take in lodgers and don't act as doorkeeper."

"But how do your lodgers go in and out Mrs Jones, surely you don't give all and sundry a key to your front door?"

"Corse not. In this neighbourhood? They have to knock to get in but I don't see them going out and I don't ask Nellie, who mostly answers the door to keep a tally."

"Did Mr Shaffer give you notice of leaving?"

"No he didn't. Just called down the area one evenin' that he would give up the room that day and asked how much he owed. I told him a weeks rent. He paid up, already had two bags with him and orf he went."

"Two bags you say. Presumably one was the carpet bag, what was the other like?"

"A bit like one of those doctors bags. I hadn't seen him with that one before."

"And how did he pay you, Mrs Jones?"

"Three half-crowns, a week's rent."

"I don't suppose you have any of those half-crowns still, Mrs Jones?"

"After three weeks? What do you think? I just get by as it is, paying the rent for the whole house and not always getting my money in. There ain't no spare for savings spite what a lot round here might think."

George tried to diffuse this anger by murmuring quietly " I understand Mrs Jones. Did Mr Shaffer leave anything behind by chance."

It didn't work. The woman obviously thought that this was a trick question and that she was being accused of something.

"What do you mean? Left something behind that I have kept?"

George rushed along. "I was not thinking of anything of value Mrs Jones and to be honest I have no idea what I meant. It came to me that perhaps he left something behind in the room which you came across after he was gone. A book perhaps, a piece of paper even, or a railway ticket, bits and pieces that you would not keep but that you might remember."

Mollified, Sarah Jones replied that she came across nothing like that.

"Is the room occupied now, Mrs Jones?"

"No, it is not. You can see it if you like but there is nothing left in it from before. In fact there's less cos my last lodger nicked a blanket so you can see why I don't keep half-crowns for long."

The room was small, with a bed, a small table and a smaller dresser with two drawers. Nobody stayed long here he surmised. This was not a home just a port in a storm perhaps.

"Before I go, Mrs Jones, I know you did not interfere in your lodgers' affairs but did you get the impression that he knew anyone hereabouts, have visitors of any kind?"

"I don't remember any visitors and he left the house usually in the morning and came back in the evenings but I doubt if he knew anyone in the square."

George decided that there was little more to be found out about this mysterious Shaffer or Da Silva or Sylvester in these lodgings. What was clear was that he ensured that he left as little trace as possible wherever he was, including changing his name as regularly as his underwear or even more so.

34

Back then to Wellclose Square and the lodgings of the former acquaintance of Sylvester as no doubt he would have been known to the now missing Mr Partner. George wondered if this was also a false name. Aliases seem to keep coming up all the time in this enquiry.

The door was opened by a middle-aged woman and George explained his purpose.

Fortunately the man used the same name in these lodgings as he had at his employment at the bank, so there was no need for too much in the way of explanation and hopefully, there was not going to be too much mysterious lack of information.

The woman immediately invited him in and took him into what was obviously her parlour with a seat in the window where she could see the comings and goings of her lodgers.

"What can you tell me about Mr Partner? Mrs?"

The double question was answered as he hoped.

"I am Edith Watson, constable and I can tell you little of Mr Partner. His first name was Edward as he told it to me, he lodged here for three months. A respectable man working in a bank in the city."

"Did he have visitors?"

"Not many, but then he appeared to work long hours for a bank clerk, but then he may not have come straight home after finishing work."

"What do you mean by that, Mrs Watson?"

"Only that he went out at about eight in the morning and presumably worked until five or six in the evening. I assume those are normal hours for a bank but did not usually get home until gone ten in the evening. I guessed that he met friends in the meantime and perhaps had a meal with them before coming home. I didn't ask."

To constantly come up against this always self-proclaimed reluctance to enquire into lodgers business was difficult to deal with. As a lodger himself he hoped that it was true, but from experience, he knew that it was not. Landladies professed to respect their lodgers' privacy but that did not prevent them from garnering every scrap of information that they could over the period of time of a tenancy.

Oh well press on and see where it took him.

"What about locally, Mrs Watson? Did he associate with anyone locally as far as you know?"

"As I said, he came home late of weekdays and had few visitors that I can recall, and none from around here."

George knew that any visitors would be well remembered by this sharp lady.

He produced the picture of the dead man. "Do you recall seeing this man at all. Either visiting Mr Partner or in the vicinity?"

"Well he certainly looks like a man who came here a couple of times, usually on a Sunday and once he and Mr Partner went out together after he called round. I got the impression that he lived not far away."

"When did Mr Partner leave? Did he give you notice?"

"No. That was the odd thing. I thought he was settled here, a steady job in a bank and did not have much in the way of visitors. But one day he said that he was transferred to a branch in Ireland and had to go immediately. With that, one Saturday it was, he packed his bags. Paid me to the end of the month which was more than I was expecting and was gone."

"Did he leave anything behind? I mean did he take everything with him, nothing to be forwarded later?"

"No that was the other thing. When I went into his room later I half expected there to be stuff that he had not taken with him but there was nothing. Not even an old newspaper or book or whatever. He didn't need to buy any furniture for himself so there would have been nothing like that, but somehow it all seemed so empty really that I wondered if he had been planning on leaving before and got ready for it."

"What about Wiltons, Round the corner. Did he go there?"

"I have no idea. I do not frequent places like that myself so I would not have seen him there."

"You say that he said he was going to Ireland. Was he Irish do you know?"

"Not sure. There are a lot of paddys around here and he did not sound like them, but then sometimes he did. He sounded more like an American that stayed here a year or two ago, but of course I can't be certain because I did not ask."

"What about when he first came. Did you ask him where he came from then?"

"I don't remember that much. I had a card in the window and he knocked and said a friend told him about it. He seemed respectable, said he worked in a bank and that was that."

"Forgive me for asking this Mrs Watson and I know little about the business of letting out rooms but are you not taking a risk in allowing anyone to come and rent a room in your house without wanting to know more about them?"

"I go on instinct, constable. I have been letting rooms in this house for more than twenty years and I think I am a good judge. Haven't been wrong yet."

George could not but think that her first mistake in judging character could well be her last if she was murdered in her bed by a previously unknown lodger.

There did not seem to be much point in asking to see the room as there was nothing left behind, so he took his leave.

As he left the house he noticed what he thought was a familiar structure on one side of the square. He walked over to it and obviously it was the old watchhouse. Unused like the one in Bermondsey with a rusting padlock on the door. He had the key to the other padlock in his pocket and on a whim, he found that it fitted this one. It opened with some difficulty, but he managed it and pushed open the door. Almost identical in size to the south London one but no bodies and no indication that it had been used for many years.

Was this a coincidence? Something to ponder on as he made his way back to the other side of the river and more familiar territory.

36

George decided to resume his usual cautious mode and returned to his lodgings to change into his uniform. It was now midday and he was not sure what instructions, if any, had been left for him at the station.

Inspector Brannan was not normally at the station on a Saturday afternoon but it was on this occasion so George went straight in to see him to give a verbal report on his morning's visits.

"Can't help saying Morrison, that all you have brought back is more mystery than real information that will move us along in the actual murder. All of this would no doubt be useful for whoever is supposed to be investigating these forgeries and it may well be proof of a link to other matters."

"What other matters are they sir?"

"Not necessarily relevant to the murder, Morrison, so we can leave them aside. We still have to concentrate on that and we are no further forward as I said. Nothing of what you have discovered gives us an inkling of a motive, although the disappearance of this Partner to Ireland at about the same time is suspicious. Perhaps we should try to find out more about this chap in case he is actually the murderer and has decamped as a result. We need more information from the bank, they will have references from when he first went there but they are closed now so that will have to wait until Monday. Perhaps Mr Brunswick knows more than he told us before and I want another word with him anyway. You and I, Morrison, will take a stroll over there now and see if he is at home."

Brannan was not one to stand on ceremony in Police matters no matter what airs and graces these banking folk might give themselves. He did not even consider the possibility that Saturday afternoon might not be a convenient time to call.

The door was answered by a young woman they had not seen before. Obviously a maid, so there had been changes in the household in the last week. Seeing the policeman in uniform and assuming that the other was his superior she invited them in and asked them to wait in the hallway whilst she informed the Brunswicks of their presence. Must be new to this job thought Morrison and will no doubt get a telling off after they had gone.

She returned and showed them into the parlour and said that Mr Brunswick would be with them shortly.

Another little bit of asserting that he was superior to policemen, even an Inspector. Morrison never ceased to find amusement in these mores of the middling classes.

Brunswick came into the room dressed in a maroon smoking jacket and a light coloured pair of trousers incongruously paired with some fur lined slippers.

"I was not expecting to see you again Inspector I am sure I have given you all the information that I have regarding Mr Sylvester."

"Perhaps you have Mr Brunswick, but it is about Mr Partner that I have called today."

In the absence of an invitation to sit Brannan took the initiative to force some civility out of this man and said: "May I sit here?"

"Of course Inspector. I will not be able to tell you much about Partner. What is it you wished to know?"

"You said that he was a colleague so perhaps you could run down what you know of him, how long you had known him, where he was from, did he have relatives and so on."

"To start with the last part, Inspector I know nothing of his personal life as we did not socialise. He was not exactly a colleague either, he came to the bank to carry out an audit of certain accounts on behalf of a client and was permitted by the management to use a room at the bank for that purpose. He brought documents with him to the office which he compared with the relevant ledgers of three accounts relating to Irish companies. This lasted a few weeks as far as I am aware, but he did not come every day."

"Did you not find this strange Mr Brunswick?"

"It was not my position to enquire into that and in any case it was not so unusual. Some customers who do not reside in London regularly employ an outside accountant to check the banks ledgers relating to their accounts. As this is a well-conducted bank the directors have no problem with allowing this providing the proper authority is provided."

"So if you did not know Mr Partner well, Sir, how was it that you accepted his recommendation of Mr Sylvester as a lodger?"

"With hindsight, Inspector, it was very lax of me. I must confess that sometimes when one meets a respectable professional person on a regular basis, at work, it is easy to forget that you do not know anything about them. This was the case with Mr Partner. He was affable, well dressed, knew his business so therefore in my eyes there was no reason to question his suggestion Mr Sylvester as a suitable lodger."

"Do you have any idea who his employer was or the accounts that he audited and to what end?"

"As I said in hindsight, these are things perhaps I should have known, but as a supervising accountant, I am not cognisant with all the accounts that the bank holds. When you asked for his address I found only one letter on file. It was from a small Irish Bank requesting the facility to allow Mr Partner to compare our ledger with documents he would produce. The letter gave his address but did not give the names of the accounts."

"Then how did your directors know which accounts to allow him to see."

"As I said, Inspector, this was a common practice in banking for out of town clients. An auditor would be given the use of a room for a few days and a clerk assigned to produce the ledgers requested. In almost every instance that I have been aware of the authorising letter gave details of the accounts to be inspected. In this instance, there was a lapse and it did not happen. Not only that, I spoke to the clerk concerned who told me that he had assumed that there was authority for the accounts requested. He did not keep a list of those inspected by Mr Partner and did not remember them."

"Why could he not remember them?"

"We use account numbers in our bank, Inspector, rather than names, so if Partner requested an account by number the clerk would not necessarily look at the name so therefore not remember it."

"No log book of the accounts requested?"

"No Inspector. The banking system is built on trust by necessity. Our customers need to trust us and we have to make it perfectly clear that we trust them. It is imperative in that situation to place as little impediments in the way of conducting banking business as we can. To the outsider, this may appear to be lax, but it is not. Trust both ways is essential. It is unlikely that Mr Partner was not who he claimed to be, so any suspicion in that direction, I am sure will be found to be wrong."

"That's as may be, Mr Brunswick. If I have the time I will certainly test your hypothesis. Going back to Mr Sylvester. You accepted him on face value also but it would appear that he was not as respectable as you thought. I cannot go into details but we need to know more about his time here. It would be helpful if over the next couple of days you could discuss this with your wife and make a note of exactly when you first met, when he came to live here and the dates, if possible, when he was away. You could also ask your maid and the cook about this as well."

Seeing that Brunswick was about to protest, Brannan continued.

"I realise that you will regard this as an imposition, Mr Brunswick, and I agree that it is. But I am hoping that you will accept that it is necessary if we are going to discover who is responsible for his death."

"Very well Inspector, I will do as you say."

"Before I go, Sir, I see that there is a different young woman answering your door. Is the other one no longer in your employ?"

"No she found herself another post and we have engaged Mary full time so that my wife does not need to see callers at the front door."

"Thank you then, sir. I presume you have been notified to attend the resumed inquest on Monday, so I shall see you there and hopefully, you will have had the time to give me a written note of what I have asked."

Morrison then spoke for the first time since entering the room. "I have been told today, Sir, that Mr Sylvester was in possession of two bags at his previous lodgings. Do you recall if he had both whilst he was staying here?"

Brunswick did not even look at the constable and addressed his reply to the Inspector. "Inspector, I have said on numerous occasions that I saw little of our lodger and certainly did not inspect his luggage. However I will include the constable's question in my discussion with my wife."

George was not particularly put down by this patent snub. It was an attitude that he had become accustomed to almost from his first day in the police force.

They took their leave with no more said. Morrison was relieved, having stood for most of the time without saying a word. He had made numerous notes in his pocketbook, even though the Inspector had not requested it. It was fortunate that he had learned shorthand writing as a youngster. It was not exactly the same as any other practitioner, but was accurate enough for his own purposes and even after several weeks he could still read what he had written.

36

Their walk back to the station was started in silence. Brannan had still not completely confided in Morrison about the instructions from above and was reluctant to tell him too much about his misgivings on the trend of the enquiry.

"So what was that about the two bags then?"

"I did mention it in my report at the station, Sir. The landlady in Stepney said he had two bags but we have seen only one. It could be important to know if the second bag ever came to Admiral Square and if it did, where is it?"

"I agree. So what do you think Morrison?"

"About what sir?"

"About our Mr Brunswick for a start. The fact that he took in a lodger on the sayso of someone he hardly knew even though he originally claimed that it was a colleague."

"He claims that the banking system is based on trust Sir, Well some would believe that, but I would not. There was something strange about the whole story that bank directors would let someone come in to their bank with only an unverified letter of introduction and go through accounts just like that. If it is true then I would not like to have any money in a bank like that."

"I agree Morrison. That really is where the whole mystery of where Sylvester or Da Silva comes from begins. But is his death anything to do with all this?"

"I do not see how it cannot be Sir. It's true that the random murder cannot be completely ruled out, but it seems more and more unlikely. There is almost a roll call of unexplained facts and missing items"

They arrived back at the station and George went into the back room to write up his report of his enquiries this morning and to make a summary of the meeting with Brunswick in the afternoon, in case the inspector did not make one of his own.

Returning to the Inspector's office, George handed over the sheaf of papers and asked if he was required any more that day.

"You can go home now Morrison, but I will be back here in the morning despite it being a Sunday. You come in to see me at ten o'clock and I will decide if there is anything that can be done tomorrow. I will tell the Sergeant to leave you off the roster until further notice. I am hoping that the inquest will be concluded on Monday and we will then be free to conclude this enquiry one way or another."

Brannan did not admit to the constable that he had no idea what to do next. Morrison had been correct in saying that there were too many unexplained bits of evidence, but how to go about getting an explanation? This whole thing had been muddied by the interference of the Commissioner or his office, no doubt under pressure from the Mint and the Home Office. Without the suspicions of the Mint's watchers and the ownership of some fake coins, there would have been no reason to consider this murder as being anything unusual.

Perhaps that would be the way to go. Ask his father what had been the evidence for the suspicions about Sylvester or Da Silva which had caused him to be under surveillance. What did they have that linked him to the actual counterfeiting operation? So that could be the move for tomorrow. Invite himself to Sunday dinner with his parents or should he invite them to his own home?

And what to use Morrison for on a Sunday. he could well go back to Admiral Square and knock on a few doors. he could also go back to the East End and do the same there. That may produce something but then again it might not. Although not having been schooled in detective work, the Inspector was a methodical man and was of the opinion that good police work was best done with routine and the collection of facts.

There were few unexplained deaths as a normal rule in Bermondsey. Domestic violence was rife and often ended with serious injuries but there was rarely any mystery about the perpetrators. Wives killed husbands, often with good reason, but that did not save them from the rope. Brothers killed brothers, jealous husbands killed their cuckolds and strangers died in pub brawls, but there was never far to look. Detective work was hardly ever required so there was little opportunity to practice these skills. Just routine and the job was done.

This Sylvester or Da Silva death was a different kettle of fish and whilst it was obvious that young Morrison was relishing the challenge, for his own part Brannan was irritated. He could not see a clear way forward and whatever the outcome it was unlikely to be anything but messy.

Sitting in his office and musing in this way was not going to help so he quickly completed his own notes of the day's proceedings and went home for his supper.

37

The Inspector was right. George was beginning to enjoy this detective job. No routine walking the beat during the day for a few hours in the morning and then again in the afternoon or when on nights for a ten hour stint with no breaks.

Although he had always been satisfied with his decision to become a policeman and for the most part the days were varied enough not to become boring, there was still a measure of tedium creeping in sometimes.

He was not of a poetic bent but sometimes considered that perhaps a policeman's job would suit a poet. Instead of starving in a garret as happened in fiction, he could be paid to walk around the streets of the Borough, observing humanity and composing couplets or sonnets or whatever about the things that he could see. Poetry did not have to be about fields and meadows or lovesick swains, it could, and in George's eyes, perhaps should be about the lives and loves of ordinary people. Pity then he was not a poet.

By the time he got back to his digs he was beginning to notice that there had been no time for any dinner today.

So a quick wash and off down to the chop house.

The menu was much as it always was. A new proprietor had recently taken over and had begun to have "specials" which he wrote on a blackboard pinned to the door so the customers could see as they went in. There was rarely anything new, the place was a chophouse after all so lamb or mutton chops were always there so nothing special about that.

The owner's wife, though was a good cook and her meat pies were always worth having so George opted for that. Perhaps that was the real reason for the specials board, customers made quicker decisions.

His pie had not yet arrived and the policeman was nursing a pint of porter, having decided that he would just have the one this evening and return to his room after his meal. That plan was not to come to fruition when his friend, the newspaper man arrived and joined him at the table.

"I see that you were on plain clothes duty again today George. Have you been seconded to the detective branch."

George had not seen Frank at his lodgings so he wondered where he had been seen in his civilian clothes. Obviously not much of disguise if he was instantly recognised.

Frank grinned having guessed that his friend was wondering about his knowledge.

"Saw you on Fish Street Hill this morning, very dapper you were too. I couldn't speak as I was getting a good story from a fishwife and by the time I was finished you were gone. As it happened it was a story, which on reflection, I cant use, except perhaps in thirty years time in my memoirs. What about you did not get anything interesting?"

George hesitated, as he always did, but knew that his friend would not betray any confidence about the investigation so he told him of the morning's enquiries but held back about the afternoon.

"All very rum. Don't you think? George"

"Anything in particular making you say that?"

"You know how I think George. Put a lot of little bits together and it becomes a single story. The secret is in putting all the little bits in the right order. Now with this little project of yours I still can't see a pattern."

"His friends sighed "I hope you are not going to spoil my supper with a great long rambling rigmarole about my job. I have had two long walks today and I am not really in the mood."

"Come on George. You did ask. And in any case, my rigmarole might even help."

"How do you work that one out?"

"Simple. At the moment you are being a detective, even if your bosses are not calling you that. You are collecting information and as far as you are concerned you hand it in and they do the thinking. But of course you cant leave it at that, so why not use my method of producing a story, gather all your facts and try to put them in the right order."

George's meal arrived and Frank went to the counter and ordered his own, returning to the tables with two pints as he had noticed that the other's glass was nearly empty.

He allowed his friend to finish eating and when his own meal arrived he tucked in without broaching the subject of police work again.

The two meals over and the glasses once again empty there was no way in which Morrison could avoid getting in two more drinks. This would make his the third of the evening when he had intended to have only one and return to his digs. Such was life and he knew the newspaper still had a bone between his teeth and had no intention of letting the policeman leave without resuming the conversation.

"So do you want an explanation of why I thought your activities rum?"

"Whether I want one or not, no doubt you are going to tell me."

"Well you did ask. Anyway at Wiltons yesterday evening, you went off during the performance and I must admit that I would have liked to have done the same. Anyway, I saw you talking to the old chap at the counter and he appeared to be giving you directions. I didn't ask about it at the time but then today I see you obviously heading for Stepney again. Now then where you working last night without telling me and finished off whatever it was this morning?"

His friend laughed out loud.

"I thought you were a reporter, dealing in facts. Seems to me your natural bent is for fiction. Think about it. I had the evening off and suggested we went up west, but you were heading east with your sister and invited me along. How could I have known that? If I could do tricks like that I could earn money on that stage at Wiltons."

"Oh well, I grant you that. But you were working there's no two ways about that because you did ask for directions and you were off there first thing this morning. So chance then and not clairvoyance, although I think you could cut quite a figure on stage in a dinner suit and moustache claiming to read the minds of swooning young women. Susan asked about you by the way."

Not sure if to pick up on the last throwaway line he replied casually "Oh really. What was she asking?"

"The usual stuff that predatory females ask, how old you were, where you were from etcetera. Didn't need to ask about your prospects, being a bobby obviously you have none."

"Thank you very much for that vote of confidence. I could rise in the police force and the pay is not bad and in any case, I might decide not stay in. There are others things I could do."

"I was not putting you down George so don't get uppity. In fact I gave you a glowing testimonial. How well read you are, nicely spoken with good manners which of course she could tell for herself. But if you want to meet her again you will have to wait for another visit as she returns home tomorrow."

"Did she say she wanted to meet me again?"

"Not in so many words, but I think so yes. hence all the questions."

George was hoping that this conversational interlude had steered the newshound's nose away from the original conversation. He was wrong of course. Frank Evans was not to be diverted.

"Now then, what were you doing down Stepney way again this morning?"

"How do you know I was going to Stepney. As it happened the Royal Mint is in that direction."

"I know that. But you would not have needed directions to the mint whilst you are in Wiltons Music Hall in darkest Stepney."

"Well you know I cant discuss police business with you, Frank. I have told you before. Ask for an interview with Inspector Brannan and get whatever he is willing to tell you. or wait for the inquest on Monday and no doubt you will get the story then."

"It wouldn't hurt to tell me why you were over there in your own clothes. You know that I would not pass it on"

"OK. But only this. The dead man was lodging in Admiral Square and he had previously had lodgings in Stepney. He had been introduced to his landlord in Admiral Square by a colleague at his bank and this colleague also had lodgings in the East End. I made enquiries at both those addresses. Now I am sure that you will get all this information at the inquest and you can follow it up for yourself if you feel so inclined, after that."

"Right I accept that but there is something that I know in my bones that I am not going to get at the inquest. Why are you doing the enquiries over there, in your own clothes and not the local men?"

"All I am going to say about that, and please be careful how you mention this if you do. These are instructions from above that the enquiry is to be kept routine but special measures can be taken. And seriously that is all I know. And please do not use that phrase to anyone."

"Right. You have my word. I am going to think out loud but don't answer. It will probably be disjointed because I will not have everything in order.

One. Murdered man in Bermondsey watchhouse but not necessarily killed there.

Two. Has connections with dud coins.

Three. Previously in the east end.

Four. The interest of police hierarchy and possibly Royal Mint.

Five. Only routine enquiries to make it look as though being dealt with as a common murder, possibly robbery gone wrong, but it isn't.

Six. What was he doing in watchhouse? A meeting or was body dumped there?

Seven. Death connected with dud coins or something more personal?

I must write all this down because I am getting lost."

The policeman stood up preparing to depart. "Frank I think you are right. Have you heard of the oozlum bird?"

"No."

"I thought that you too was well read. Apparently, the oozlum bird flies round in ever diminishing circles until it disappears up its own backside. I fear you are in danger of doing that."

"Don't go off like that George and I am serious. Think about my method and you will see that marshalling the facts and changing the apparent order is as suitable for solving a crime as it is for writing a newspaper report."

The policeman resumed his seat. "I was just pulling your leg Frank and I accept that your method could have merit for a detective. But I am not a detective and the problem that I would have in using your system is that I do not have all the facts. And that is where you have the advantage. You can surmise what you do not know but a policeman has to stick to what he does know."

"I disagree and we could stay here all night discussing this but I know that you probably have an early start tomorrow. But I will say this and ask you to think about it. There is no reason why a policeman cannot look at the facts that he has and surmise about the ones that he does not have. He can then test the surmises, or theories if you like and look for evidence to support them. For instance, there has to be a motive for every human action, criminal or otherwise. The facts may not point to a motive but there will be one there so it may be necessary to guess, surmise or theorise about a motive and test those that you come up with."

"I told you that you were tending towards fiction writing, Frank. Perhaps that is going to be your forte in the future. I will think about what you have said but now I must go. As you say I have an early start and no means of knowing how long a day it is going to be. My bones tell me that it is going to be a long one."

38

Sunday morning and bells of St. John Horsleydown church woke him from his sleep. His pocket watch told him that it was already ten minutes to nine and the bells were ringing for the nine-o'clock service. He had overslept but fortunately he was not due in to see the inspector until ten. That extra pint of porter will need to be avoided in future, he could not afford to be this late on a normal day.

Inspector Brannan was already at the station when the constable arrived a little earlier than he had been instructed but that did not stop the superior criticising him for being late.

George knew better than to dispute this. He had thought that ten o'clock was a little late for starting a policeman's day but nonetheless he had assumed that the inspector had his reasons.

"Right Morrison, your tasks for today are to go to Admiral Square and knock on some doors to see if anything else can be gleaned there. You will have to use your initiative to decide when you have gained enough and then go back to Stepney and do the same there. We need to be ready for the inquest tomorrow and have answers to any questions that the coroner might throw at us before deciding on a verdict."

George pointed out that he would need to be in uniform in the division so should he stay in uniform when he went to the other side of the river.

"Good point. Go home and change into your own clothes before going to Admiral Square, no civilian is going to argue that you should be in uniform but you can then go straight over to Stepney."

Morrison left to do as he bid and Brannan left the office to visit his parents in Finsbury. He had decided against making it a meal visit and if he left now he would catch them before they went to morning service.

39

Admiral Square was quiet in the Sunday morning light with a few children playing in the gardens in the centre, but very little other signs of life.

George decided to knock on the door of Mrs Henderson's house to see the maid and enquire if it would be convenient to speak to the lady of the house.

Alice welcomed him with a smile and made no comment about his civilian clothes, so he thought that his morning would not be wasted. But business first. Mrs Henderson agreed to see him but was not as welcoming.

"I thought, constable that I made it clear that I would contact you if I decided to confide my reasons for visiting Mrs Brunswick."

"You did madam and I am not here to press you on that point. It occurred to me that as an observant person you could be well placed to supply some information about your other neighbours. It is not gossip that I am asking for but an assessment, if you will, of anyone else living in the square who may, even by chance, have made contact with the dead man."

"Not very subtle, constable" she smiled. "You are not asking for gossip but you would like some. Or are you asking me to be a detective?"

"I am not even a detective myself, Mrs Henderson. Its that I thought that as a literary person you would observe the people that you see and meet in a somewhat different light than other ladies."

"I am not sure if that was intended to be flattering, constable Morrison, but I will accept is as such."

Morrison did not reply, waiting to see how she would proceed.

She stood and went to the window and looked out for a few minutes and then turned.

"Come and look out of the window with me."

George joined her at the window and they stood side by side, looking out. He waited again for her to take the initiative.

"I understand that this area is not part of your normal beat, the most regular man is constable Evans to whom I have spoken on a few occasions. You will not therefore be familiar with the square but he will be and perhaps you should have asked him for the observations that you are asking me."

"I'm afraid that a policeman would not look at this square with the same inner eye that you would use, Madam."

"Very perceptive and of course you are right. This square is a little unusual in that it contains both old and new houses. The reason for that is that the builder who developed these two sides of the square ran out of funds before he could acquire the rest of the older houses. Some of those are in church ownership and no doubt they wanted more than forty pieces of silver." The barb in that remark was not lost on George, but he did not respond.

"As a result of this only partial development, the builder also had difficulty in disposing of some of the houses he had built. It was not going to be the middle-class community that he envisaged and there are some who do not wish to live cheek by jowl, as it were, with the working classes. Therefore the new houses on this side has become a mix of professional people who took up long leases before it became clear that the project would not continue, and others who have taken short leases, not intending to stay. I doubt if any of the people living in the old houses across the other side of the gardens would have had any contact with your dead man. There are some poets sharing a house on this side and a couple of doctors have houses. The poets I have not met and I have no need of doctors, but it is possible that your dead man may have needed medical attention and it could be worthwhile visiting them and asking. The hatters, further along have only business premises and will not be there on a Sunday morning but could be worth a visit on another day. Mr and Mrs Brunswick, you know of course. But looking around this morning I really cannot think of anyone who might have had contact with your corpse and in any case I understand that he had not been a lodger for any length of time."

"No, he had only been here a few weeks. During the time that you have been here, Mrs Henderson, have there been numerous changes of occupancy on this side of the square"

"Not numerous but certainly more than I have experienced in other similar areas. Most professional people take up relatively long leases, of five years or more, and for the most part, see the leases out before moving on. Of course I have no knowledge of the actual ownership of the houses in the square, so there could well be sub-leasing going on and even sub-sub leasing where those not wishing to live here but cannot get out of the lease will either rent out or take in lodgers."

"Thank you for your comments, madam. I apologise for disturbing you in this way, particularly on a Sunday morning"

"I have not been disturbed, constable and Sundays have no more significance to me than any other day. I please myself on what I do on every day of the week."

George wished that he had that freedom himself but knew better than to express that opinion.

The other calls in the square produced nothing of interest, the doctors knew nothing and the poets were still in their beds.

As he was about to leave the square, having seen nothing of his colleague Evans he saw Mrs Brunswick leaving her house and getting into a hansom cab. It was something in the way that she carried herself, which he did not notice before, which reminded him of some of the performers at Wiltons music hall. Could she be the young actress in the carte de visite? Is that why that face seemed familiar to him?

40

James Brannan, former Inspector in the detective branch of the Metropolitan police was having the last cup of coffee of his breakfast when his son arrived.

There was still coffee in the pot so the Inspector was able to join his father and sat with him in the breakfast room of the house in Radnor Street, Finsbury

"Well now James, it is not filial duty which brings you here on this Sunday morning even though it is a while since you visited your mother."

"I accept your admonishment on that score, but I am sure that mother well appreciates that is lack of time rather than affection which delays our family visits. You are correct though in your assessment that this is almost an official visit, albeit on a Sunday morning. We have not made any real progress on the murder and I wished to ask for all the information you can give me on the antecedents of the dead man, in case his death has nothing to do with the coining."

"You are certainly correct in taking that possibility into account. I have a file here which you are welcome to peruse, but I need to keep it here as I have a meeting tomorrow at the Mint and will need it there."

"I am sure that you are familiar with everything in the file so perhaps you could draw my attention to anything you consider germain, particularly how this man first came to your attention."

"I know the first part of course. It was associating with two known criminals. Although we call the men in my team watchers in fact, for the most part they are listeners. These two men had been making enquiries about a supply of fake coins and were later seen on several occasions with this Da Silva apparently discussing some kind of deal. So Da Sylva was watched."

"Was there any reason to connect any of these men, Da Silva and the other two to the recent spate of these good fakes, if you can use this term?"

"Not at the beginning, and in any case these fakes are not as recent as you suppose. We cannot know for sure how long they have been in circulation and this is because they are good, so there is no means of knowing how many are in the hands of the general population without being detected."

"But the connection with da Silva?"

"That's even more questionable. He has been watched, as closely as we can for coming up to three months. Obviously twenty-four hour surveillance is not possible with our resources but about eight weeks ago, he was followed to Liverpool and shortly after that there were reports from the banks in Liverpool of the fakes turning up there."

"Why the banks and not the police."

"Come on James. You know that the police only become involved if there is a complaint from a shopkeeper or publican that an individual has tried to pass a dud coin. This is not happening with these coins. For the most part they are only detected in the banking system. Obviously, there is a smart distribution system going on here. They are fed into the purses of ordinary citizens in some way which still leaves a profit for the coiners. It is clear that there are large numbers going round and round without being noticed. It is only when a large shop decides to bank surplus coinage that they are being picked up. By that time there is no way of knowing how they got into the system."

"So Da Silva goes to Liverpool and then there is a spate of coins being detected. Could be a coincidence., Are you aware of a parallel occurrence?"

"Yes. Birmingham earlier but we did not see the connection at the time."

"But if he is the courier surely one of your watchers should have noticed him carrying heavy baggage."

"We don't think he is the actual courier nor is he the mastermind, but he is involved somehow. His supposed background as a metallurgist makes him suspect as being part of the manufacturing process."

"So how do you see the connection with his trips to places where the coins later appear."

"Using guesswork it is easy to suppose that if he is a senior partner in this enterprise then he could go ahead to either set up a distribution network or to make contact with one of the criminal gangs in the provinces to arrange for them to deal with the distribution."

"Feasible, I suppose, and then the consignments go along later."

"That's how I see it anyway"

"None of this helps me with this murder though. If there was a successful operation going on then we are unlikely to be dealing with a falling out of thieves so his death may not be connected to that."

"I agree." The older man responded, "and there will be the need to look for another motive."

"Going back to the coining. Have you made no progress in finding the factory?"

"None whatsoever. There are thousands of small workshops in back alleys, arches and semi derelict warehouses where such an operation could be going on. Finding one in particular without informants is an impossible task. We may get lucky but I am not holding my breath."

"Now about these two herberts that he was seen with on this side of the river. Are they still about?"

"As far as I know. We cant keep every known forger under surveillance all the time, let alone any on the edges, as it were. I don't have the men."

"Well, I will need to talk to them. I can't ignore the fact that they knew the dead man. It is difficult enough getting a handle on him as it is."

"I could have him delivered to you at the Borough if you like."

The inspector showed his surprise, but his father just grinned at that.

"Come on James. My men are not policemen as I have reminded you before. I will see what I can lay on. If possible, tomorrow."

"I would be grateful for that. I will need to get everything I can from them, and inside a cell will be the best place."

"Do you think that we have not tried that for information about the forgeries? They know nothing. They were only prospective contacts."

"I will still need to get all they know about the man."

The inspector rose to his feet "Well thank you for all of that, even if it doesn't move me further forward for the moment. I will not delay you further this morning."

"Your mother is in the kitchen, James, You will speak with her before you leave and perhaps make an arrangement for you both to come for a proper visit."

41

Once again dressed in his own suit Morrison had a brisk walk back to Stepney, using the same route as before. He noticed that the door to Wiltons music Hall was open so went in.

It was quite dark inside and Morrison called out to find if anyone was around. The old man he spoke to previously emerged from the gloom at the rear asked what he wanted.

George reminded him of his previous visit and the discussion about the cartes de visite. Still being reluctant to part with sixpence he asked to see the one of the young actress they discussed earlier to remind himself.

The old man produced the cards from a box under the desk and spread several out like a pack of playing cards. "See if you can remember." he grinned.

Joining in Morrison responded "That's not fair, it's as black as Newgate's knocker in here. Anyway, they all look alike when they are up there on the stage. Difficult to know one from another, so its the same in these cards."

"That's not true. These are good likenesses of them without the stage make-up, so if you knew 'em you could tell."

"That is still a big proviso. I have to know them before being able to recognise them. So seeing a picture is not really going to be able to help me recognise one of them in the street."

"That's as maybe, constable. But it is still better than no picture at all."

George peered closely at the faces of the women and was still sure that the standard poses made it difficult to tell one from another. Perhaps he was wrong in thinking that he recognised a face. He chose one and was wrong, it was not Lily Laverne. The old man picked out the correct card and told him to take it to the door to confirm. The wintry sunlight was sufficient for him to see that there was a similarity to Mrs Brunswick but perhaps it was only superficial.

He thanked the man for his trouble and resumed his journey to Wellclose Square.

He doubted the value of this expedition right from the beginning. This was a rundown area although the sizes of the houses indicated that it had seen better times and probably had some fairly well to do occupants in the past. The old church standing in the centre of the square was now used as a hostel for Danish and Norwegian seamen and on this Sunday morning there were clusters of men sitting about in the yard smoking and talking. There was no point in trying to talk to them, George knew from his beat in

Bermondsey that foreign seamen rarely bothered to learn English. Why should they? For the most part they worked on vessels mastered by their own countrymen and so could understand orders given on board.

George decided to choose the side of the square opposite the one where the mysterious Partner lodged. Number one Wellclose Square he found was divided into no less than seven separate tenancies. After speaking to two of the householders, if they could be called that, in a house where seventeen people lived in six rooms, he was confirmed in his opinion of the futility of this exercise, working alone. He discovered the occupancy of the house from John Murphy who told him that he was a chemists assistant and described the families who lived in the house in great detail. |He was also able to tell Morrison about most of the other houses on this side of the square. He could not recognise the man in the drawing and explained that although he knew most of the families who were his neighbours he did not see many visitors to the square due to the long hours that he worked. Murphy was not Irish, despite his name and said that he came from Gloucestershire, a part of the country never visited by Morrison.

The constable decided to skip the next few houses, in view of Murphy's description and went to another side of the square.

He was aware that he was not doing this job well. No doubt because of his inner feeling that it was a non-productive exercise. It was expecting close to a miracle to find someone in this overcrowded area who may have seen the two men together. It could happen in fiction, of course, but not in real life.

The next two calls were much the same, except he did not come across anyone as expansive and knowledgeable as Murphy. Most of the men looked at him with suspicion and after giving a glance at the drawing quickly gave a shake of the head and closed the door. The women for the most part gave the impression of looking more closely at the image but still denied having seen the man in the square.

Morrison was prepared to admit, if only to himself, that the beard and moustache sported by so many men, even among the labouring classes, made it difficult to tell one from another. When he thought about his own acquaintances he had to admit that quite often it was small things, facial expressions, eye colour and so on which helped recognition. More often than not it was clothing. He knew a man's suit sometimes better than the wearers face.

He decided to move on to Princes Square. The Inspector had not been specific as to how long he should spend in the area or how many people he needed to interview in the hope of getting information.

Morrison quite liked Inspector Brannan and knew that he was a good policeman, but he wondered about his handling of this enquiry. Morrison had no training in detective work and doubted if the Inspector had either. Come to think of it, was there any training in detection of crime? He mulled this over as he walked and decided that he would divert down to the Highway in hope of finding a coffee shop open, it was a long time since his meagre breakfast. Although he passed a street stall selling coffee on his previous visit, he was not keen on standing in the street drinking coffee. In any case he needed a sit down. He was young and fairly fit, used to long hours on his feet, but sometimes everyone finds the need of a chair.

He was lucky there was a corner shop open with the name Cohen over the door and he went in and ordered a coffee. He was also able to order a bagle with some salt beef inside which would keep him going until he could go off duty later and get a meal. There were not many other customers at this time on a Sunday afternoon and George wondered if this was due to the day and the time or the bitterness of the coffee. It was of the strong American variety which was becoming popular and George was still undecided about it suiting his taste.

He found himself a seat near the window so that he could watch the passers-by. A policeman's habit which he deliberately cultivated. He was not sure why but thought he read somewhere that it was a good mental exercise to look closely at people to observe their clothing, mannerisms, a way of walking and so on, the easier to be able to recall them later.

George was well aware that his mind was a ragbag of information, much of it being of very little practical use whatsoever. He wondered about Mrs Henderson, the writer, did she do the same when she was collecting material for her books. When he had the time he would try to find a book by the lady to see what it was that she wrote about. If he was been bolder he could ask to borrow one, but that was not his way.

One of the things about coffee shops was that it was rare to be pressured to leave after finishing what you had purchased and he was suddenly aware that he had been sitting, observing and musing for far too long and had best be on his way.

42

Princes Square looked no different today than yesterday. There was no indication of an afternoon service at the Swedish church sitting in the centre of the square surrounded by iron railings enclosing the graveyard. In fact there were very little human activity at all. It was not cold and it would have been normal in a similar area in Bermondsey for street urchins to be playing in the street and for groups of housewives to be congregating discussing whatever housewives discussed when there were more than three together. George guessed that for the most part the talk would be about someone who wasn't present.

There were three women talking together outside one of the houses adjacent to the one that he visited previously so this could as good a place as any. The eldest of the three women moved off as he approached.

The two females were about the same height, not very tall but slim and pleasantly faced. One was perhaps a couple of years older than the other. They were not dressed in any

"Sunday best" but possibly in the clothes they would wear for work, depending on the job.

"Good afternoon ladies, I am a police officer from Southwark and I wonder if you could help me."

The elder of the two, though probably no more than twenty years of age responded by hardening her face and almost spat "Why should we?"

"Because I assume that you would have no reason not to. If, though, you do have a reason for not wishing to speak to a policeman just to answer some simple questions which will not be about yourself then I will draw my own conclusions."

"And then?"

"And then, I will leave, but have words with the local patrol and suggest that they keep and eye on you."

"All right then. What do you want?

"If you would be so good as to look at this drawing and tell me if you ever saw this man in the square. Quite simple really and not affecting you in any way."

The women looked at the drawing and then at each other.

"Well, what do you think? Did you see him hereabouts?"

"Oh yes ,we saw him. Dint we Dolly?"

Oh dear thought George this is going to be like drawing teeth. He hated having this situation with women. He knew he had taken a risk with pushing back at the initial response, but thankfully it worked. But now..

"Do you want to tell me about it?"

"Well we dint like him" responded Dolly

"For a reason?"

"Oh yes. a bloody good reason. He took it that if you dint work during the day then you worked at night if you know what I mean."

"I understand. Did this cause problems for you?"

"Corse it did. We both worked in the mat factory down the 'ighway which caught fire a month or so ago and aint worked regular since apart from morning cleanin. This cove kept coming up to us every time he saw us in the square of an evening and asked us where our room was. We knew what 'e ment and we are not like that."

"So how did you deal with him?"

"Told him to shove off else I would put me bruvver on him"

"And did you?"

"What?"

"Put your brother on him?"

She laughed then for the first time in the conversation "I ain't got one. But 'e didn't know that did 'e"

"So he shoved off. What about other women in the square. Did he bother anyone else as far as you know?"

"Only Maggie at number twenty-one, She's only sixteen and lives with her gran."

"Look, I am sorry if we got off on the wrong foot and I think that what you have told me could be important so if you don't mind giving me your names and where you live I may need to send an Inspector to talk to you."

"Who is this cove, then?"

"He was found dead last week in Bermondsey."

"We don't want to get involved in anyfing like that."

"You wont be involved because it happened in Bermondsey but what you have told be could be important."

The both acquiesced and George noted the names and the house number in his notebook, thanked them for their help and proceeded immediately to number 21.

Fortunately, Maggie and her gran lived on the ground floor so were not difficult to find and they were both at home.

He would have preferred to have spoken to the girl alone in case she had not told her grandmother about the incidents with the dead man. However, sometimes you have to take things as they are.

The girl had, in fact told the grandmother what had happened with the man so she was able to discuss it openly.

"Maggie, how many times did this man approach you and what were you doing at the time?"

The girl thought for a while and then responded slowly. "Two or three times, or perhaps just two 'cos the third time I avoided him but he was going to speak to me."

"What time of day and what were you doing.?"

"It was evenings, not sure of time of course we don't 'ave a clock. Each time I was going down to the Prince for a quartern of ale for gran. I did think the last time that he was waiting for me."

"And what did he say to you the first time? Can you remember?"

"Not exactly. Sumfin about where I worked. I dint answer and just walked on. Gran says not to talk to strange men."

"So you thought he was strange. Why was that? He lived round here so you may have seen him before."

"Don't remember seeing im before. Anyway, he was shifty and had a funny look."

George decided not to pursue a description of the funny look for the time being.

"And what about the next time?"

"Same fing really. Except he stood in front of me and I had to stop. So I told him I didn't work round here and hoisted up the jug as if to lump him one and he moved out of the way."

"Had you any idea why he might have approached you?"

"Corse I did. I'm not a kid you know. I know what goes on and in any case I told Dolly about it and she told me to be careful of 'im."

"Did he appear threatening in any way?"

"No, not really. Better dressed than most of the coves round here so praps he thought 'e could come on to me."

The grandmother had been sitting in the corner all this time and had not spoken. She was not really old and had an intelligent gleam in her eye.

"What about you, gran? Did you see any of this?"

The old woman accepted the familiarity without comment.

"Can't see much in the dark from here. But I watched out after Maggie told me about the first time and saw that she dealt with it the second time. So I was not concerned. There are always folk about in the square so nothing could have happened as long as she kept in view. We all know each other here."

"But you didn't know this man even though he lived across the square."

"No we dint know him, but I made it my business to find out that he lived with Sarah Jones, 'adnt bin there long and 'ad a good job somewhere no one knew"

"Tell me. Does this sort of thing go on all the time?"

"What sort of thing?"

"Strangers accosting young women in the street."

"I thought you said you were a policeman. Corse it does. It goes on everywhere. Men of all kinds think that they have only to flash a shilling or even less at any girl and she will do what he wants. You must know that. Cant imagine it is not the same in Bermondsey."

George felt the need to defend himself. "Of course I know it goes on. But I thought that perhaps in a square like this, everyone knowing everyone else that it would have been less likely."

"Squares ain't no different to anywhere else. Don't forget we sit tween the ighway and Cable Street. There are all the paid off seamen around as well as the toffs looking for what they regard as a bit of rough. Most of the local men, of course know better than to try it on here so no doubt they go elsewhere. Men are like that no matter where you are."

This last tirade was without a smile. The old woman clearly had strong views on the subject.

It was clear that little more could be learned here but he told them both that he may have to come back if his inspector had further questions.

It was time now to make his way back to Southwark and see if the inspector was still at the station. That was another part of his instructions that had not been made clear, so discretion was called for. Back home to change in to uniform and then to the station to either report verbally or make out a written report which in the circumstances was going to take some time. Most of the information gained today would need to be considered as possibly providing a motive for the murder which had not been apparent before.

If Sylvester had been regularly approaching young women then he could have come across a prostitute whose pimp took umbrage about something. This happened all too often but usually only ended in injury to the prospective client but not murder.

43

Passing Wiltons Music Hall once more he thought that he could enquiry about this Lily one more time and see if the porter knew if it was her real name. Once again he wished that he had come more prepared for this task. He should have asked the first time. He knew that people on the stage regularly did not use there own names.

The old man came from the back as he had before, "You again, young man."

"Yes. I forgot to ask, was Lily Laverne her real name?

"No idea, but unlikely."

"How can I find out?"

"Aint no lists as far as I know. The performing folk most often choose a name for themselves for when they are on the stage so that when it is over they can go back to being themselves."

"Would Mr Wilton know, do you think? Is he here?"

"He's here, Finishing auditioning some new artistes. He may know so I will go and ask him. Look after the desk for me will you?"

He soon returned and said, "Mr Wilton will see you for a few moments."

The backstage office was quite large and was well furnished. Morrison was taken aback by the sight of John Wilton who displayed perhaps the largest set of mutton-chop whiskers he had ever seen. Of course, he could make no comment on them.

"Williams says that you are interested in Lily Laverne. Can you tell me why?"

"Only, sir, that she resembles someone involved in an enquiry in Bermondsey and as other people involved have lived in this area of Stepney in the past I wondered about a connection."

"Logical, I suppose. You wonder if Lily Laverne is her real name?"

"Well sir, if it is not, then it would be helpful if I did know what her real name is, and where she might be now."

"I do not think it is her real name. She came here soon after I reopened this Hall, auditioned as a solo artiste, singing sentimental ballads which are popular. She was pretty, her voice although not strong could carry to the back of the hall so I gave her a try.

She was quite popular although she had difficulty in handling some of the lewd comments from the young men so was easily put off. She eventually told me that she had decided that this area of work was not for her and she would try for more serious parts as an actress.

As for her real name. I have no idea. It was not Lily Laverne of course, but she could have been Polly Perkins for all I know. There is no need for us to know the personal lives of performers. It is what they do on stage that matters."

"Have you any idea if she was successful in obtaining a part in a dramatic performance?"

"No idea, but I doubt it. As I said, a pretty little singer who could have done well on the halls if she had learned to adapt. But there was no indication of any great dramatic qualities. But then who am I to judge? I do not need dramatic performances here at my music hall. I need entertainers, and that is what I get."

"Well thank you for your time, Mr Wilton, it has been a pleasure meeting you."

"If you want a copy of the carte of Lily, tell Williams that you may have one gratis."

"Thank you very much, sir. That will be most helpful."

It was quite dark by the time he got out into the gloom of Graces Alley so he set off back to Bermondsey, and hoped that by the time he arrived at the Borough police station the Inspector would have gone home to his loving wife and his supper.

44

He still hadn't decided if to go straight to the station or go home and change. He was still not sure how many of the men at the station would be aware of his present duties and how many of those would be aware of his civilian clothes status.

So safe side again. If the Inspector did not wish it generally known about the civilian clothes then he must needs turn up in uniform.

George had prepared his report in his head on the way back from the east end and decided not to mention Lily Laverne

The Inspector was still there even though it was close to six o'clock when he arrived back. He was clearly impatient, told Morrison to sit and get on with a verbal report of his days enquiries.

George decided on a chronological resume of his calls at the houses in Wellclose squarer and Princes Square and of finding no one who actually knew either of the two men. When it came to Sylvester's alleged approaches to the young women he emphasised the predatory nature of the encounters.

"Apart from Sylvester approaching young women and girls in the way you have mentioned there is little more that moves us forward."

"May I suggest sir that if he carried on in the same way in this division, then he could have fallen foul of a pimp and thus ended up with a beating which went too far."

"Still stretching conjecture a bit far, Morrison and doesn't explain the coining."

"There may not be a connection sir."

"There may not be a connection, Morrison, but our superiors think there is. Ours not to reason why. Write up your report and leave it on my desk and go home. Be back first thing in the morning, there is the resumed inquest to attend."

45

His salt beef bagel in the Jewish coffee shop seemed hours away by the time George got back to his digs.

The specials menu at the chop house beckoned and although he knew that he risked being bearded by his friend the newspaper reporter he decided to go and get a meal.

True enough soon after placing his order and sitting down with a pint of porter on the table, Frank Evans sat down opposite him.

George looked across at him and spoke first. "I sometimes wonder, Frank, if you do not have some kind of pigeon in your ancestry. It is quite uncanny how you manage to home into me almost every time that I come and sit on this seat."

His friend laughed aloud. "I like that George. I must try to remember to use it in my memoirs. Or perhaps use it in my biography of you as the great detective."

"Please don't keep on about that Frank. It is no longer funny."

"Sorry my friend. I am not actually taking the rise out of you. You are currently employed as a detective even though you are not a member of the illustrious, or perhaps not so illustrious, detective branch. And I am quite sure that you are taking the job very seriously, and I will not be surprised if you do not come up with a result. Eventually."

"That's as may be."

Then on a whim, he produced the photograph of Lily Laverne from his pocket.

" Do you recall having seen this lady before?"

"A carte de visite of an actress or performer in your pocket George! What is the world coming too? No I have not seen this lady perform or seen her elsewhere. Why do you ask? Is she connected with your investigation?"

"I am not sure. I am not even sure if in fact she is one of the people connected with the dead man. These are such small photographs and it is not easy to make out details, especially when they are specially posed. I think I know her from somewhere but am not certain."

"So what do you want me to do?"

"I presume you will be attending the resumed inquest tomorrow. So perhaps you could keep an eye on those attending and let me know if you think she is there. A long shot and even if she is the person I am thinking of it may not be significant."

"Surely if this Lily Laverne turns up at the inquest it has got to be significant?"

"Perhaps, but then perhaps not."

"So what did Brannan think of this Lily Laverne?"

"I didn't tell him."

"Not very wise George. Withholding evidence and all that."

"I am not withholding evidence. I saw this photograph at Wiltons and thought that it resembled someone here in Bermondsey. Until I know for sure then it is not evidence of anything. I can't go to the Inspector with every supposition that I make. That is not my role. You forget I am a foot soldier in this police force. Not expected to have any brains let alone think about anything."

The reporter sighed. " You are right of course. One of those facts which may not be a fact that we were talking about before. I was not sure about attending the inquest but I will do so. Even if it will only last ten minutes like so many of the inquests conducted by this vain coroner of ours."

46

Inspector Brannan had only been in the police station fifteen minutes when the Superintendent walked in and sat in his usual seat at the side.

"Right Brannan, have you prepared a resume of the evidence I shall be giving at the inquest today?"

"I do not recall that you advised me that you had intended to present the police evidence. I assumed that as this was supposed to be a routine enquiry then it would have been myself or one of the sergeants doing that."

The superintendent stood up, tucked his hands into the tails of his frock coat and almost theatrically paced around the room.

"I have read the brief reports you have sent to my office this week on the progress or lack of it in this investigation. Whilst from a police service point of view it is less than satisfactory, for the purposes of our superiors it may all be to the good. They clearly want no fuss about this death and a simple murder verdict from the inquest would leave us clear to continue enquiries on the coining aspect without fuss or pressure."

"But surely Superintendent, your appearing at the inquest to present the police evidence could possibly mitigate against that. You are quite well known and the coroner, being inclined to be somewhat erratic in his cases on this side of the river could easily decide that there is more to this and pursue a line of questioning which might be awkward."

"I am quite capable of dealing with awkward questions from this coroner, and in any case, I had intended to have a quiet word with him beforehand."

Brannan was well aware of the convoluted relationships amongst senior members of the police force, the judiciary and other parts of the legal system so would not be surprised that a "quiet word beforehand" could be expected to achieve the result required.

"As you wish, Superintendent. We have an hour or more before we need to proceed to the hospital for the inquest. I will write you out a statement of the facts that we have elicited about the dead man. We have found no evidence of malice towards him which could explain his death so this should be sufficient for the coroner to advise the jury on a murder by persons unknown verdict."

"Very well. I will return to my office. Have your report there within the hour and I will see you again at the inquest."

Brannan looked down at this desk and by the time he raised his eyes again his superior had gone.

47

The contingent from the Borough police station arrived at the hospital where the inquest was to be held in the library.

The superintendent was already there and so was Mr and Mrs Brunswick and Frank Evans, Morrison noted that Mrs Henderson had also decided to attend, perhaps out of curiosity or then again collecting material for whatever the book was that she was writing at the moment.

There was no set form for the conduct of inquests. It was entirely up to the coroner and they all had different methods.

The jury was the same twelve men who had been there the previous week and the coroner began by reminding them of the evidence they had heard then.

He then called the Superintendent to present the evidence of the enquiries that had been made buy the police during the previous week.

He kept it brief. Recounted the various names that the man had used at his different addresses but that no one could be found who could supply a motive for his murder. Made no mention of counterfeit coins.

At first, it appeared that the quiet word that the Superintendent had hoped would keep the proceeding brief was not to have worked.

"Surely Superintendent, if this man used false names, then he must have had criminal connections?"

"It does not necessarily follow, Sir. There are a number of perfectly valid reasons for a respectable person to use a nom de plume as it were. Use of a name other than your own is not evidence of criminal intent. Suspicions of course, but not evidence."

"Very well, I will accept that. Are you satisfied that sufficient enquiries have been made by your officers to find witnesses to the event itself?"

"Yes Sir. You may recall the weather during the few days prior to the discovery of the body was bad so that there were few people abroad at night time who may have seen something significant."

"Thank you, Superintendent. I may ask you some more questions later."

Mr Brunswick was then called to give evidence. He told the coroner the same story that he had given to the police. He knew nothing of the man before he became a lodger and his absence from the house was assumed to be in connection with a business trip.

The coroner questioned the advisability of taking in lodgers that were complete strangers and Mr Brunswick agreed that with hindsight it had been.

George Morrison was looking at Mrs Brunswick all the time that her husband was giving his evidence. He was sure that she was afraid that she herself would also be called and there were a range of emotions going across her face. He was also sure, at the end, that she was Lily Laverne in a previous life. Now how was he going to deal with that?

Almost abruptly the coroner turned to the jury and said "You have heard the evidence that no one can be identified as being responsible for the death of this man, whatever his real name is. You will have no alternative but to bring in a verdict of murder by persons unknown. The foreman of the jury stood and agreed.

The coroner rose from his seat and left the room and that was that.

Morrison hurried from the room in order to catch Evans before he left the building. He had no need to hurry, his friend was waiting in a corner.

"What do you think?" he whispered.

"What about?"

"Don't mess about Frank. I haven't got much time. Did you see Lily Laverne in the room?"

"Of course I did. It was the wife of the bloke where the dead guy was lodging. No doubt in my mind. So what do you think is the connection?"

There was no time to reply as there was a bark from Sergeant Brewer and George knew that he had to come to heel. "Will try to see you this evening. You try and get a statement from the Super or the Inspector but don't push it or they will think I have been telling you things."

"What did that newspaper man want Morrison?"

"We live in the same house, Sarge. Just passing the time of day. In any case he was waiting for the Super."

"What for?"

George had to bite his tongue. At times this sergeant could ask the most stupid questions.

"Because he works for a newspaper, Sarge. The Super has given evidence so he wants a story. That's what they are like. The inquest itself is never enough."

"I hope you have not been giving him stories."

"He is not interested in stories from police constables, Sarge. Not juicy enough. Has to be someone important, so they can make up a headline."

On their way back to the station Morrison asked if the sergeant had been given any instructions about returning him to the roster.

"No, I haven't. The last order was off roster till further notice. So that is what we do in this service. Just like the army. It is the last order that counts, so you stay doing that until you are told to do something different. Makes life simple really. Cant go wrong whilst obeying the last order."

Morrison was well aware of this philosophy of the sergeant's but could not recall that he had ever heard it put in so many words.

48

The Superintendent and Inspector left the inquest room together and Brannan waited for the other to speak first.

"I am back to my office now, Brannan. Send me a note of what you intend to do now so I can keep the commissioner up to date."

Brannan could barely contain his impatience.

"You have no instructions, then Sir?"

"Why should I Inspector? It's your enquiry. Good day."

So this was how it was going to proceed, arms length, do it by the book, use your initiative until it goes wrong. Why was he surprised? Even his use of a constable in civilian clothes could be questioned in the future as he had received no specific instructions to ignore the rule about wearing uniform at all times.

Whilst the inquest verdict had not been a surprise Brannan had not actually prepared a plan of action to follow-up Morrison's report of his enquiries in the east end. It was all a bit confusing. The east end angle was really related to the coining and not necessarily the murder. So it should be back to the murder and finding a motive. But what motive if it was not related to the coining?

Brannan smiled to himself at the recollection of the way in which the super had turned aside the question about false names being evidence of criminality. Who did he think he was going to kid with that response? But the coroner appeared to accept it so perhaps the "quiet word" had worked after all.

Perhaps it was back to Admiral Square. He wondered if he could persuade the super to apply for a search warrant. But on what grounds? They would have to reveal to the magistrate the connecting with counterfeit coins so no doubt the super would have to refer up to the commissioner's office for permission to apply. Perhaps after a week or so since the actual death there not be anything to find anyway. But what if there is?

Frank Evans caught up with Brannan as he walked along St. Thomas Street.

"Inspector, can you tell me anything about how your enquiries into the murder are proceeding?"

"No. You know me better than that Mr Evans. If you want a statement come to the station and ask for an interview. Don't try to interview me in the street. That will not work with me."

"My apologies, Inspector. But I know how busy you are so I thought perhaps you could give me some indication of the lines you are working on to discover the criminal?"

"That's still asking for an interview. And I do not do interviews in the street."

By this time they had got to Borough High Street and were in view of the station.

"One last thing then Inspector. Not for publication. Why did the Superintendent give the police evidence?"

"Because he chose to. That is what Superintendents do. Now for publication, enquiries are continuing and when we have any information to disclose to a newspaper a statement will be made. Good morning Mr Evans. Don't come in now and ask for an appointment as you will not get one. As you so rightly noticed I am a busy man."

49

Reluctant as he was to accept the point of view of the Super about the enquiry, Brannan knew that there was no alternative but to pursue the murder enquiry in the ordinary way. He was coming to the conclusion that the coining aspect had diverted their attention to the east end of London to no avail. Nothing Morrison had reported had any bearing on the murder, except possibly for the fact that the man had approached young women.

These concerns were put to one side as he was advised that he had two visitors in the cells.

So his father had succeeded in persuading the two contacts of Da Silva in the east end to venture south of the river.

Brannan was not generally inclined to make assumptions on appearances, but on this occasion he could not prevent the thought that these two looked like criminals.

Two youngish men in their late twenties, dressed in a flashy sort of way which indicated to the Inspector that they were not gainfully employed in any manual occupation. No employment at all, probably, except for their criminal activities. The Inspector was prepared to accept that these were involved in coining even if they did not make any forgeries themselves. Most coining was a cottage industry conducted by unskilled folk who had been shown what to do, or had only watched it being done and coming to the conclusion that it was easy money.

Brewer was close behind him as he looked at the two men in the cell.

"Is there anything in particular that you would like me to ask these two gentlemen, Sir?"

"Thank you Sergeant. At first, I will just talk to these two myself and see if they are prepared to volunteer the information that we need,"

Brewer considered that this would be a waste of time and that persuasion would be necessary, so why not start with that?

The two men sat on the cell bed attached to the wall and Brewer produced a chair for the inspector to sit on.

"Now then you two. First your names."

The slightly older of the two, still cocky despite being in a police cell, most likely not for the first time, responded: "Why are we here."

"You are here because I want you here and I am asking the questions. So tell us your names and then we can move on."

They both mumbled names, Smith and Brown. which no doubt were false, but Brewer noted them down anyway.

"Right" continued the inspector, ignoring the names, that didnt matter at this stage. Their true names could be obtained later if it was necessary.

Showing the two a copy of the image of the dead man he asked: "What do you know of this man we found dead hereabouts last week?"

The older one answered again "Don't know him"

"That is surprising. A man you saw on several occasions, who called himself Da Silva amongst other things and you don't remember him?"

"Didn't know he was dead."

"Well he is, Had his head bashed in. So what do you know about that?

"What do you mean? We didn't know he was dead."

"What I mean is. A man you knew well but claim not to know is found dead. You two are known for violence so you had better tell us all you know about him before I decide to charge you with his murder."

"We don't know anything about him. Met him a month or two ago. He came to us and we had not known him before."

"So what kind of proposition did he come to you with?"

"Didn't come clean at first, but then said he had a load of sovs to sell at a good price. Didn't show us any though just half-crowns which were good."

"Did you buy any sovs?"

"No, cos he didn't have any and we thought the half-crowns might not have been kosher either."

"In what way?"

"Come on you must know the score. He might have been setting us up. He could have showed us genuine half-crowns and claimed they were what he was making then unloaded a load of crap on us."

"But you still saw him several times."

"Yes well if he was on the up, it could have been a good thing for us, but we needed to be sure."

"So you checked him out."

"Sort of."

"So what did you find out?"

The younger of the two who had claimed that his name was Brown then joined the conversation for the first time.

"He was cagey and didn't let much slip. Says he was a trained chemist or something from Birmingham and had the means to produce good amounts of coins in a factory and not just back street stuff."

"Was he from Birmingham?"

"Dunno. Odd accent, not London but don't know from where."

"Irish?"

"Nah. For crying out loud, we would know a paddy a mile off. But never knew anyone from up north so don't know what they sound like."

"So what happened? Why no deal?"

"Dunno. He just didn't turn up anymore."

"But over a month or more you surely found out more about him than that. Had he approached anyone else that you knew? And how come he came to you?"

"He didn't say why he came to us.

"And you didn't ask? Don't come the acid with me, you two. You are sharper than that and unless you come up with a better story than so far you are going to stay in this cell."

Smith responded very quickly but to still deny that they knew any more.

"We told you. He came out of the blue. Seemed to know about us but no one else knew anything about him. We found no one else that he had spoken to. So we got nowhere with finding out about him. We had pretty much given up the idea of going along with him anyway when he didn't turn up no more."

"I am curious as to why he chose you two without anyone in the area knowing him. What do you two do for a living?

"We collect rents."

"Rents or debts?"

"Both if need be. But we're not bully boys if that's what you are coming to. Most of our clients are respectable landlords, we just collect the rents and few don't pay up, so its easy money with no bother."

"So what about the coining?"

"We are not involved in coining. It's a mugs game. A lot of work for bugger all return and the risk of being picked up every time you pass a dud. Not worth it."

"So why did he come to you?"

"We thought perhaps that it was because we handle a fair bit of dosh. Pay it into the bank for clients. So could slip the moodys into the real cash gradually and less chance of being noticed."

"Sounds reasonable. So whoever put him on to you could have been one of your client landlords or one of your tenants."

"Suppose."

"Right then. I presume you can write as you need to keep a record of all your collections. Got your books on you have you?"

"Corse not."

"You will have to work from memory then, and don't leave anything out. Sergeant Brewer will give you a pencil and a piece of paper and I want a list of all your landlords."

"Cant do that. Confidential see."

"That's a shame then. You will have to stay here until I search your digs and find your books which will give me what I want., And more besides I wouldn't wonder."

"You cant do that."

"Of course I can. You are murder suspects. And whilst we are on the subject of murder where were the pair of you two weeks ago?"

"What days?"

"Every day."

"Mondays we chase up any rents we couldn't get at the weekend. Tuesdays we settle up with the landlords who want cash and then bank the rest. Wednesday we went up to Chelmsford for the races and stayed till Friday night. Have to back for Saturday to collect the rents."

Where did you stay in Chelmsford?"

"Station hotel. Always stay there. They know us."

"I am sure they do."

Without waiting for any further reply Brannan left the cell and Brewer followed him.

"Leave them to stew for an hour or so, Sergeant and then see if they have changed their minds about the list."

Brewer was of the opinion that it needn't take that amount of time but said nothing. He didn't understand this softly spoken way of getting information from known criminals. But still this was the Inspector's way and there was nothing he could do about it all the time Brannan was in the station. After he had gone home then the old methods could be used.

50

Back in Admiral square again under instructions to complete another door knocking exercise with Constable Green Morrison thought he could take the opportunity of another call at the house of Mrs Henderson.

Alice answered the kitchen door as usual and greeted him with a smile.

"Another official call I'm afraid Alice."

"I've been watching you going around the square and wondered if you would include us."

"Well, here I am."

"You could have sent constable Green."

"And miss seeing you?"

"Would that have been so bad?"

"It would have been. But I still need to ask if your mistress will see me."

"You could have come to the front door."

"Yes I could have, but I am sure that Mrs Henderson would prefer that I came in this way, as I do myself."

George was quietly amazed that he had got this far in a conversation with a pretty young woman without becoming tongue-tied. But then again this was mainly official.

The girl left the kitchen but soon returned and told him to go up to the front parlour.

Mrs Henderson was seated at her desk in the window and had obviously observed his arrival. Fortunate then he had not dallied too long with Alice.

"I did not expect to see you again, constable, as this is not your area."

"I am still involved in the enquiry into the death of Mrs Brunswick's lodger and that is the reason for my visit."

"Why so, constable? I told you that I could not discuss my private conversations with Mrs Brunswick."

" You have told me that, Mrs Henderson, and I respect your reasons. However further information has come to light which may change your mind about the need for confidentiality."

He produced the carte de visite of Lily Laverne from inside his notebook and handed it to Mrs Henderson. She was not noticeably taken aback but was surprised.

"Where did you get this card, constable and why show it to me?"

"The card is among the collection of former artistes at Wiltons Music Hall in east London and I am showing it to you to ask if you recognise this Lily Laverne."

"Please do not take me for a fool constable. You know full well that this is Mrs Brunswick but what has her former occupation to do with me or your enquiries?"

"I am well aware madam that you are no fool. I showed you the photograph to obtain confirmation from you that Mrs Brunswick was Lily Laverne. Was her former occupation the subject of one of your conversations with her?"

"Yes, it was. I recognised her from a visit I had made to Wiltons Music Hall and she agreed to tell me about life behind the scenes, as it were. She agreed to this on the basis that I did not disclose her former occupation to anyone else. So I have not done so. Not that I believe that being a music hall artiste is in any way disreputable, despite the attitude in many circles. But I do understand that the wife of a bank accountant could wish not to be identified as having a former activity like that."

"Did she give you any reason why she had not pursued her career on the stage?"

"I have already told you, Constable that I will not discuss my conversations with Mrs Brunswick as I gave her my word on that."

"Very well madam. Thank you anyway for your confirmation of her identity, but I am afraid that when I ask Mrs Brunswick the same question, she may well assume that you have broken that confidence."

"So she may. And I will be sorry about that. But she will have to think what she will. For my part I know that I have not disclosed what I promised not to discuss."

The interview was obviously over. A pity that the previous rapport with this lady had now dissipated as he would probably find it difficult to have further excuses for calling and seeing Alice again. He would have like to ask the girl about her time off, but did not know how to broach the subject. And his private life was secondary to the problem he now faced of advising the Inspector of information that it would appear that he had withheld.

51

As anticipated Brannan hit the roof. George had prepared his verbal report but asked the Inspector if he wanted a written one first.

"You can do the writing later. Just tell me if you have discovered anything this afternoon which moves us forward."

George had decided to get the worst bit over first so told of the carte de visite and his proof that Mrs Brunswick had a connection with the same area of east London that the dead man had come from.

"Why didn't you mention this before the inquest?"

"Because I was not sure, Sir. These photographic images are often manipulated so that they are flattering to the person portrayed but then not a good likeness. I have little experience of actresses but I am sure that from a distance they all look alike."

"I am sure my experience of actresses is even less than yours if you are in the habit of visiting music halls, although I can't understand how you find the time."

George let that comment pass.

Brannan did not like the Brunswicks and considered that the wife had been hiding something other than a dislike of the police. And the explanation of how they took in the lodger did not hold water. Perhaps a search warrant could be justified now but it was probably too late. If in the unlikely event the murder had taken place in the house then all trace of it would have been cleaned up by now.

"It's getting late now, Morrison, write up your report of what you have found but no speculation included. Then you can be off home and be back here by eight in the morning. And none of this is to be discussed with that newspaper friend of yours. I gave him a flea in his ear this morning and he must learn nothing more than what he learned at the inquest. If there is anything in the connection you have been making, and I am not saying that there is, then it needs careful handling. Evidence is what we need.

52

Having received confirmation of the identity of Lily Laverne from Frank after the inquest then George was in no position to avoid meeting him at the chop house that evening.

"So what's new," the reporter asked as he took his seat opposite the constable.

"What's new is that I am under strict instructions not to talk to you about this case"

"I half expected that. I think I upset your inspector by bearding him in the street after he'd had words with the superintendent"

"I don't suppose you have ever found him amenable anyway."

"That's not true. I have spoken to him a number of times but always in the station and asked for an appointment rather than go straight in. I will have to remember that in future.

On a side issue as it were. I know that this actress is only the landlady as it were so you should be able to talk about that."

"Well I cant. I told the inspector about my suspicions when I got back from Admiral square this afternoon, of course he complained that I didn't tell him before but hopeful he will let that slide if something comes it."

"What do you expect to come from it."

"To be honest I have no idea. He is probably going to go home and think about it.

"Will you be going back to see her again."

"I am not sure but I think it very likely that the inspector will want to go and see her again and very soon. Carrying on from that Frank, do you go to the music hall a great deal?

"My dear George, I rarely have the time to go out of an evening for pleasure. Over the last few years I have probably visited the theatre or music hall no more than half a dozen times. Why do you ask?"

"Just wondered if you may have seen her at some time.

"Not that I recall. Do you know if she played anywhere other than Wiltons?"

"Mr Wilton thought not."

" Do you know what her real name is or is she really Lily Laverne?"

"I doubt if Lily Laverne is her real name and Mr Wilton thought the same. If it is not then I don't know what her name was. As far as we are concerned she is Rose Brunswick and her maiden name is not relevant."

"Well George, as a reporter I find maiden names to be quite often relevant and as I have mentioned before our jobs are not that different apart from the fact that I can wander off my beat. It won't be difficult to discover her maiden name and it could prove interesting."

53

Brannan did not wait for Morrison to finish his written report, but tucked the case folder under his arm and set off for home.

He'd had enough police routine for the day and decided to go home for his supper and browse through the folder quietly this evening.

As he did so, nothing new came to mind. He was still undecided about what line to take next. There were far too many strands to this investigation and he was tempted to follow Morrison's cue and seriously consider that this was not related to the coining and set it aside for the time being. After all, presumably his father and his men employed by the mint were still working on the case so they could turn something up. No sense in duplicating work. But then again their efforts before the murder were not impressive. They had let Da Silva slip through their fingers and it was only chance that the dead man had been identified. The more he thought about it the more he was convinced that this was the way to go. But which way.

One of the unresolved aspects of this man Da Sylva or Sylvester was what was he doing in Southwark and why living with the Brunswicks.? Was it just chance or was it organised? And this man Partner, who was he? and what was he doing at the bank and why did he disappear just at what might have been a crucial time?

And was the fact that Mrs Brunswick was formerly Lily Laverne, a music hall performer relevant to any of it?

A visit to the bank where Brunswick worked and a discussion with the management might be useful. There was no great rush so perhaps a letter to the bank in Dublin could bring results within a reasonable time. It would be quicker to go to Dublin himself but he doubted that it would be authorised. Relations between the police in London and those in Dublin were not cordial at the best of times because of the suspected Fenian activity. Visiting Dublin without going to the police first would be out of the question and the Superintendent would almost certainly not sanction it. He would first refer it to the Commissioner who would then refer it to the Home Office. A week could go by before permission, if any, came through. Whereas he would be entitled to write a letter to the bank and hope for a speedy response.

54

Brannan's wife, Frances rarely made any comment about his police work, she would sit on the opposite side of the fireplace crocheting or knitting whilst he sat for the most part just thinking. He was not a reader, had no time for modern novels and only occasionally purchased a newspaper. The work of a police inspector these days was mainly administrative and he often brought files home and made notes for himself of actions for the following days.

He had placed the murder file aside and just sat thinking about the possible courses of action without making any notes.

"A penny for them dear, or is it police business?"

"I am sorry my dear. I do neglect you, don't I? I sit here thinking about work, when this should be our time together."

"I have never thought that you neglected me, James. I knew your background before we married so I am not surprised to be married to a policeman."

"I know that Frances, but I should not bring my work home."

"I don't mind James. I realise that you have to have time for thinking and I am well aware that a police station is not the place for that. Too much going on at the same time. From some of the reports in the newspapers, it seems to me that more policemen should spend some time thinking instead of acting rashly and arresting people who are too often found to be innocent."

"Well that may be true, and by the same token, I may sometimes be too slow to act. But one has to tread carefully these days with one's superiors so I find it better to try to look ahead to possible consequences of any action."

"Do you want to share your thoughts, or would you like me to pour you a glass of whisky and put them aside for the rest of the evening."

"Well Frances, perhaps I shall have a whisky but I will ask for your opinion on something I learned today."

He waited for his wife to pour him the drink whilst she had a glass of sherry for herself.

"Do you know anything about the music hall, Frances?"

"What a strange question, James. You must know that I have never been to a music hall in my life. I was barely eighteen when we married, so how could a go to a music hall before that and we have not been to one together."

"Well perhaps that was a stupid question, my dear. But what do you know of the music hall and its performers?"

"Very little, apart from what I would presume is common knowledge. There are quite a few music halls in the east end of London and the provinces and there are several on this side of the river including one here in Camberwell and another in Southwark. As for the performers I only know what I have read in the newspapers and the advertisements that I have seen. Some of the performers are well known, even famous and paid a lot more money than a police inspector."

"How on earth do you know what they are paid?"

"I told you it is in the newspapers. There is one man mentioned recently as being paid thirty pounds a week which is more than you earn in a month."

"Well leaving the amount of money being earned aside. What about female performers? Are they as well paid and famous?

"I have not thought a great deal about that but I think that it is unlikely. This is a man's world after all!"

Brannan chose to ignore that final barb. His wife was of an independent frame of mind and often voiced the view what whilst slavery of black people had been abolished thirty years ago, it still continued for white married females.

"So in your newspaper articles and womens' magazines, how are female performers regarded by women generally? Are they approved of or despised as being not quite respectable, as it were. And are music hall performers looked upon differently to those in the legitimate theatre?

"If I had known that you had wanted me to carry out this research for you James, I would have come better prepared for this inquisition" she responded with a smile.

"However I can say with some assurance that the music hall is never, ever, mentioned in Mrs Beetons magazine. Especially since they put the price up. Uplifting stories, recipes for meals, patterns for knitting and so on. Nothing in the least frivolous or even remotely unsavoury"

"So the music hall is unsavoury?"

"I did not say that or intend it because I have no personal knowledge. There are some who consider all dramatic performances ungenteel whereas they are considered quite acceptable, even by the queen."

"The queen went to the music hall?"

"I thought that this was a serious discussion, James, related to your police work so please do not be frivolous."

"I am sorry Frances. I could not resist the thought of her majesty attending the music hall in happier times coming into my mind."

"Well to continue. Before the death of Prince Albert and allowing for her royal duties I am surprised that you did not know that the queen regular attended public performances of both plays and the opera. So there is nothing disreputable about either of those forms of theatre."

"But the same cannot be said for the music hall?"

"As I have said. I have never been to the music hall and it is not a subject that is mentioned in the magazines that I read. The newspapers, however often contain commentary on various aspects of the music hall. Mention of new halls being opened, the activities and salaries of famous performers and so on. It is apparent that for the most part, the performances are of a mostly very light nature of popular songs, dances, conjurors and acrobats and so on to appeal to ordinary working people."

Brannan digested this for a few moments and then said. "I think that it is time for us to attend a music hall. This is an area of our experience which is obviously lacking and needs to be remedied. When shall we go?"

"You constantly amaze me, James. Not with this proposal but by your lack of knowledge which I would have thought as a policeman you would be cognisant. There are numerous music halls on both sides of the river and new ones being opened or public houses adapted all the time. There are also several theatres within your division, the Surrey comes to mind and I would have thought that you would be familiar with all this. Since becoming an Inspector you would appear to have dropped the acute habit of observation which you used when you were a constable on the beat. May I suggest that as a policeman this is not progress."

"I accept your criticism my dear, but I hope that you will confine that opinion to these four walls. You may well be right and it is something that I will need to think about."

"I am sorry James. I should not have said that. How you do your work is none of my business."

"No Frances. You are right. Perhaps I have become so tied up in the administrative work of the station that I have forgotten that I am actually a policeman, even though I no longer walk the streets, observing, as you so rightly say."

55

Arriving early enough to get a letter in the post to the bank in Dublin he knew that it would arrive there this evening.

Despite the mounting list of things that he needed to attend to at the station Brannan decided to get the visit to Brunswick's bank out of the way and leave administration to the afternoon.

Off to the Leadenhall street for some words with the management about their seemingly lax behaviour with the visits of this man Partner.

Brannan was shown into a large office where a large man in morning suit sat behind one of the largest desks the policeman had ever seen.

"I understand that you are an inspector of the Metropolitan Police, Mr Brannan, whereas the City of London police has jurisdiction in this area."

"That is correct sir, but jurisdiction refers to where crimes are committed and I am concerned with a crime that was committed in Southwark."

"I see, then tell me how I can help you."

"Your accountant, Mr Brunswick, told me during our enquiries that a man, who is now dead, was introduced to him by a Mr Partner who was spending time here carrying out an audit of certain accounts. I have been unable to establish the connection between Mr Partner and the dead man and wondered if you had any conversation with him whilst he was here that might shed some light on the matter."

"No, I cannot, Inspector. I did not meet Mr Partner and after Mr Brunswick told me of your initial enquiry I established that only two members of staff had actually spoken to him. Mr Brunswick and the senior clerk who gave him access to accounts that he requested."

"What about when he first arrived with his letter of introduction?"

"Even then. His letter of introduction was given to me, it appeared to be in order, we had received similar requests in the past, so I gave instructions for his visit to be facilitated in the usual way. I did not meet him."

"Was it normal for letters of introduction to be presented in this way without any means of identifying the person presenting it?"

"There is no normal in these situations. It is quite common to receive these requests from out of town banks. But there is no standard form of letter. Some go into a great deal of detail as to the reasons for the request and the identity of the person to carry out the inspection. Others are very brief. Quite often the accountant or whoever bringing the letter is already known to us as a member of a firm in the city. Others come from the town where the requesting bank is located, so they are not known to us. We assume that they are known to their clients."

Brannan would have liked to stay and debated this laxity in allowing unknown persons to have access to private records but recognised that it would be futile.

"Perhaps, Sir, I could be permitted a few words with the senior clerk who dealt with Mr Partner and then I will take up no more of your time."

The banker assented with a nod, rang a brass hand bell on his desk and immediately the door was opened by a clerk who received instructions to take Brannan to see the senior clerk.

Neither Brannan nor the banker spoke again.

The senior clerk was a small waspish man with wire-framed spectacles and who appeared to be almost strangled by his wing collar, his voice coming out reedy and quiet.

"What can I tell you, sir?"

"This Mr Partner who came here a couple of months ago to inspect some accounts. Did he seem the usual type of person who came to the bank to carry out inspections?"

"I am not sure what you mean?"

"Please don't try to prevaricate. Your director has given me permission to speak to you, so you, in turn have permission to speak."

"I had no intention of prevaricating Inspector. I really did not understand what it was you wanted me to say."

"Let me put it another way then, Mr.? I presume you normally deal with most of the accountants and so on who come here on a similar mission so I also then presume that you are familiar with them. Was Mr Partner the same kind of person or did you get any impression at all that he was in any way different?"

"I am Reginald Simons, Inspector. For the most part, he certainly appeared to be carrying out an accounting function on the few accounts that he requested. However, there were certain aspects of his work that were different. He appeared to be more interested in the nature and source of the entries rather than the figures themselves. And he seemed to cover up what he had written whenever I approached."

"So what did you deduce from that Mr Simons?"

"It is not my place to deduce anything, Inspector, but did think that perhaps he was a policeman rather than an accountant hence his interest in names rather than money. But of course, I could be wrong."

"Did you draw the attention of any of your management to this apparent anomaly.?"

"No, Inspector. It was only a suspicion. In any case, he was here for only three or four days in total and by the time my impressions of his activities had been formulated he stated that he was finished and left. There was no point in mentioning them thereafter."

"I understand that there is no log or record kept of the visits of these inspecting accountants but have you any recollection of any of the names involved?"

"As you say, there is no log or record of the requests relating to numbered accounts. If Mr Partner had not known the account number and the name he would not have been given access. That is self-evident."

"So he gave the account number and the name?"

"Yes"

"And when he gave you the account number and the name did you write them down or rely on your memory."

"Naturally I wrote them down. The account numbers have both numerals and letters. They are not easy to carry in one's head back to the main index for checking."

"A notebook?"

Simons produced a small leather-bound notebook from his pocket, thumbed through several pages and began to recite a number before Brannon interrupted.

"Just write the details of all the accounts that you gave him access to Mr Simons."

All the names were clearly Irish.

Brannan did not wish to risk a rebuff by requesting to see these accounts himself and he doubted if he would quickly spot what the mysterious Partner was looking for. If necessary he could come back with someone more qualified.

56

The reply from the Eiran Bank in Dublin arrived the following morning. Rather more prompt than Brennan had anticipated and the contents were disturbing.

They had no knowledge of Mr Partner and had not requested any inspections in the city of London.

A visit to Scotland Yard then was in order. Brennan had had previous dealings with Detective Sergeant Clarke and was aware that he specialised in keeping an eye on foreign spies and possible insurgents. In this instance his special knowledge of Fenian activity could well come in useful and perhaps Partner was in reality a Scotland Yard detective or even an Irish detective in London without the knowledge of the Metropolitan Police.

Brennan had been to Scotland Yard previously and had no difficulty in contacting Clarke.

He gave the names of the three account holders who had been investigated at the Bank. and was advised all three were known to Clarke and then Brennan dropped his bombshell.

"These three all have accounts at a city bank which have been investigated by a detective. One of yours?"

"Not that I am aware and I am reasonably certain that I would have learned if it had been."

"From Ireland then? This investigator came with a false introduction from an Irish bank."

"Well if it was then again I think in the normal course of events I would still have heard about it."

"Events are not normal currently are they?"

"You could put it like that. As far as Fenian activity is concerned it appears to be centred in Ireland with the connivance of American backers, but there is still the possibility of activity on the mainland that we have yet to become aware of. The powers that be are edgy, there is no doubt and I would not put it past the Dublin Police to send one of their men over here if they got wind of these bank accounts that you mention. They have informers aplenty over there but most of what they supply is unreliable, so they could decide to check them out before sharing the information,"

"These three men. How important are they and are they here in London?"

Clarke took a large folder out of his drawer.

"The Dublin Police think that they are significant but only in Ireland but this connection with money in London could well change that perspective. It may be that it is only that money is being funnelled through London rather than any intention to use it for activities on the mainland.

What is odd is that they have used the same false names which they have used before. They must know they are known to the police in Dublin. Careless, short of forgers to create another series of false identities or just not expecting them to be found or leaked to informers."

Brannan took a chance and asked, "Sergeant have you any knowledge of the fake half-crowns being circulated that often defy detection?"

Clarke grinned. "Of course I know and so does every officer in the detective branch. The Commissioner thinks that it is a secret but it is not. This sort of thing easily circulates, why you even know about it yourself."

"To be honest, Sergeant I only know of it because of this murder, but no doubt I would have learned sooner or later."

"From a special investigator employed by the Mint possibly?"

Brennan let the implication ride. His father had been a senior detective at Scotland yard and his present employment was also well known. "Possibly. But this Irish connection to my murder may be significant and perhaps not. I needed to be clear that I would not be spoiling any investigation you were conducting before making too much fuss or taking it into account."

"Well as I have said, Inspector, there are no investigations of this nature being conducted by this branch that I am aware of. I have connections with the Dublin Police special section that deals with political activity and could discover in a couple of days for certain if it was one of their men. They should not have men on the ground in London without notifying the commissioner's office but they have been known to do that.

If it transpires that it was one of their men then I would have to advise the Commissioner, and I may well find that he knows about it. But we can cross that bridge when we come to it."

57

Brennan instructed Brewer that he was not to be disturbed unless something important like a riot outside the Borough station was taking place. And he could keep Morrison employed in the station until he was required for further enquiries on the murder.

The inspector needed to put his thoughts in order before deciding on the next step.

Perhaps the first thing was a brief note to the Superintendent would be best so as not to be accused of keeping his superior in the dark.

The note was not necessary as Horace Washington entered the room ten minutes later without knocking.

"Had no word from you inspector regarding progress on this murder and once again I am summoned to a meeting tomorrow at the Home Office. I will no doubt be asked what is happening and you have failed to tell me."

"Superintendent there has not been time to write hourly reports to you. The investigation is continuing in several areas and I had assumed that you would only wish to be informed when something significant occurred."

"Sarcasm to a superior does not become you Brennan and I do not take kindly to it. Just briefly run through the areas of your enquiry and I will decide those I need written reports on."

There was nothing for it to bring the superintendent up to date with everything that had transpired since the inquest. To deliberately omit anything at this stage which could be discovered later would be a death knell to his career if it was later found to be important.

Unusually for him, Washington sat silently through the recital and for a minute or so after Brennan also fell silent.

"At this stage whilst much of this on the surface appears to be progress, I am not sure if any is going to give you a culprit."

"I agree, sir, but this was never going to be straightforward. Although we have been tacitly permitted to go outside the division, we are hampered by being unable to make full use of local knowledge, in Stepney for instance. We may have found more there if we could have included the men on the beat in those two squares."

"That can't be helped. You were given some leeway in that respect but not carte blanche so there is no use complaining about that. The need for discretion regarding the coining was made quite clear, so that was that. At least you were able to go outside the division and use a constable in his own clothes, which is unusual."

"But we are not even sure if the coining was connected to the murder, Sir. The more information that we get even suggests that it is unlikely and there may have been another motive."

"For instance?"

"Two possible motives come to mind. The man was a sexual predator, openly approaching young women in the street and now the possible link to Fenian activity."

"I will accept the first, Brannan, but not the second. The Fenian connection to your man is tenuous to say the least."

"I agree, Sir, but there is a possible connection. If one were to create a chart of everyone we have interviewed so far all of them are linked. So there is a kind of connection with the Irish accounts at the bank and the dead man so it cannot be ignored as a possible motive. These groups fall out and when they do there is violence."

The superintendent rose. "I will call in again tomorrow before going to the Home Office and will expect to be handed a full briefing on where you are up to by then. I hope that I will not be called upon to explain lack of progress in bringing this enquiry to a conclusion."

Brannan was no longer in the mood for writing all this out. Whilst he thought that he had brought all his thoughts together for the benefit of the Superintendent, he was no longer sure that it was a coherent summary of the investigation. It was not even leading anywhere.

Perhaps a written plan of action might be more productive.

"Morrison, did you do mathematics at school?"

Morrison gave no indication that he was surprised by the question but agreed that he had.

"Good. I have had an idea of showing the connections between all the people involved in this murder enquiry. I want you to make a chart which names everyone we have interviewed between us and draw a line between all those connected to each other. Do you get the idea?"

"I do indeed sir, but how will this help in identifying the murderer?"

"I don't know that it will give us the murderer, just like that but I have a feeling that it may show us a connection we may have been missing and thus point to a motive that we have not considered before."

"Very well sir, but I may need to purchase a large sheet of paper from one of the print shops."

"Well do that then. Tell them to send us a bill."

"And I will need a list of the names that you want me to include on the chart, Sir. I am not aware of everyone you have spoken to."

"Right. Let us make the list together. Sit down, Morrison. Get out your pencil and write on this sheet here, starting with your own name and that of Mr Evans."

"Me and Evans, Sir?"

"I said that to be effective this chart will need to include everyone involved in the enquiry. You and Evans discovered the body. So start with you two and then we will go on to the victim, his landlady and her husband, his former landlady, the man who introduced them and so on until we have a complete list."

This list took almost half an hour to compile before Brennan was satisfied that it included everybody. Although it had originally been an almost throwaway line to the superintendent as they progressed down the list Brannan became more and more convinced that this could produce something useful.

They had a discussion as to whether the watchers from the Mint should be included. At first they decided against and then decided to include them as an anonymous connection but there anyway. Morrison had also had doubts about including the cook and the maids in Admiral square but had not voiced them.

By the time they had finished the list it was well into the afternoon, so Morrison was sent off to get the sheet of paper from the print shop and return to carry out the job. Neither had any idea how long the task would take.

Fortunately for Morrison he was able to make a satisfactory chart containing all the names they had discussed. Fortunately they all fitted on the newspaper - sized sheet he had obtained from the print shop. He had had the foresight to purchase two sheets in case the first did not turn out to be satisfactory.

Although he had done some elementary mathematics under the tuition of his father at the village school it had not included a great deal of geometry so Morrison had to guess at a suitable layout for the chart. He regretted not having discussed this with the inspector before leaving the office but it was too late now. so he had to make a start.

He decided to put the murdered man in the centre of the page and draw a number of squares around the edge to contain the names of the suspects. By now he was thinking along the lines that perhaps the inspector regarded everyone as a suspect.

By six o'clock he had finished and was satisfied that he had done the best that he could. He was not convinced that it was such a useful tool in the enquiry as Brannan was expecting, but that was not a constables problem.

Brannan, however appeared pleased and said that it was the kind of chart he had envisaged. he would take it home with him to study this evening and then tomorrow they would pin it on the wall and discuss its implications.

Neither made any comment on how the relationship between the inspector and the constable had changed during the course of the last few days. Brannan had obviously subconsciously decided to include Morrison in every aspect of the case and to use the younger man as a sounding board for his thoughts on the next moves to make.

58

The chart was already on the wall of the inspector's office when Morrison reported for duty.

He noticed that the inspector had drawn some additional lines on the chart, in red ink. Morrison had only used the same colour as the names and the box outlines.

The red lines connected the murdered man with both the Brunswicks that Morrison had included separately as well as the mysterious Partner. Morrison had already drawn those lines in himself as well as connecting lines between the Brunswicks and Partner. There were other lines connecting Mrs Brunswick or Lily Laverne, Partner and the two young women in Wellclose square.

Brannan had added an additional square alongside the name of the dead man. The watchhouse. Morrison saw the significance of this and mentally kicked himself for failing to included it. Of course, the location of the dead body could be a connection in itself. A meeting place or something else still unknown but needing to be considered.

"Sit down Morrison and look at the small changes I have made to your chart and admit to yourself that perhaps I was wrong in thinking that this would be helpful."

Taken by surprise the constable waited for a few moments before responding.

"Not in the least Sir. As I was creating the chart in the way that you suggested I came to the opposite conclusion. Perhaps the significance of the connections may not be immediately apparent, I think that in time more connections may well suggest themselves or even be brought to our attention."

"Perhaps you're right, Morrison. I admit that after studying it last night and making those few additions I thought that perhaps I had wasted your time and expected too much from this visual demonstration of the facts that we know."

"Well Sir, the red lines you have drawn in show a connection between both the dead man, the landlady in Admiral Square and Wellclose Square. There should also be a red line between her husband and Partner and Princes Square, and if the two squares were blocked together perhaps as Stepney that would show another link. Both the Brunswicks having a connection with the east end."

"And your conclusions from those connections?"

"No conclusions, Inspector. Just drawing attention to connections which could be lines for further enquiry. Perhaps Mr Brunswick should be called in to explain if he can."

"I had already had in mind to have that gentleman in this office to explain himself. It is obvious that he has been lying somewhere along the way and we have to know the reasons why."

"What particular lies?"

"His relationship with Partner is the main area. He told us specifically the man was a colleague and that was why he accepted his recommendation of Sylvester as a lodger. Partner was not a colleague just a short-term visitor to the bank for what at present is unknown reasons. He hardly knew the man. Why lie about that? He presumably knew even less about the man he took into his house as a lodger. Doesn't make sense, so there has to be a reason that we need to know. "

"And Mrs Brunswick?"

"I think that we will need to see her separately and perhaps today may be a good day. We can then leave a message with her for her husband to come here when he gets home."

"Will you broach the subject of her previous occupation Inspector."

"I think we must, Morrison. If we do not mention it now and only bring it up later we could be accused of being devious about it. We have some facts and need to have them explained in more detail in case they are relevant to this enquiry."

59

The maid at the Brunswick's house admitted them into the hallway and asked them to wait whilst you went in to advise her mistress of their arrival.

Mrs Brunswick appeared to be prepared for them so perhaps she saw them arrive from the front window.

"Please sit down Inspector and tell me what I can do for you."

George being a menial was expected to stand so he responded by ostentatiously taking his notebook from his pocket and pretended to test the sharpness of his pencil. This demonstration was not lost on the woman but she ignored it.

"We need to know more about the movements of Mr Sylvester whilst he was staying here. I asked your husband to discuss with you what both of you recall about that. Did you have that discussion?

"Yes, Inspector we spent almost a whole evening on the subject, although there was not a great deal that I could add to what I told you when you first came."

"Did your husband make any notes of these discussions?"

"Yes, Inspector. There was not much to it but he intended to give them to you after the Inquest but by the time we came out you were nowhere to be seen."

"Well, no matter. If the notes did not contain a great deal, then you will no doubt be able to recall what was on them."

"I will not need to recall, Inspector. The notes are here."

She got a single sheet of paper from a small bureau in a corner of the room and handed it to Brannan.

"As you say, Madam. Not a great deal of information about a man who lived under your roof for close to two months."

"I have explained on several occasions, I am sure, Inspector that I did not watch Mr Sylvester's comings and goings and held no lengthy conversations with him. He was a lodger. I am not used to having lodgers so perhaps I was more reserved than others in the same role., Nevertheless that is my nature, so that is all I know about the man and what he did or did not do whilst he lived here."

"We have been making enquiries in Stepney where your Mr Sylvester lodged prior to coming to live with you. I understand that you have also had connections in that area in the past. Did you come across Mr Sylvester there?"

"What makes you say that Inspector?"

"Well you did appear at Wilton's Music Hall, did you not and that is only a short walk from where Mr Sylvester lodged. So I wondered, given the proximity of the two places if you had seen him there.,"

"I certainly have no recollection of having seen Mr Sylvester before he came here by arrangement with my husband."

Brannan was quietly surprised by the ease in which she accepted their knowledge of her occupation as an actress and had passed it off.

"So what do you think now then, Mrs Brunswick? Was it a coincidence that Mr Sylvester may have seen your performance at Wilton's and then turns up as a possible lodger?"

"I have no means of knowing if Mr Sylvester attended Wiltons and I have not been in or near that Music Hall since my marriage. I do not know where he lodged before as I did not discuss the matter with him so was not aware of any proximity to Wiltons."

"A coincidence then?"

"One must suppose so, Inspector, without any evidence to show otherwise."

"Did you appear at any other venues, apart from Wiltons?"

"I am not sure if my theatrical career, brief as it was, is relevant to your enquiry, Inspector, but no I did not."

"As I have already pointed out, Mrs Brunswick, the seeming coincidence of the two sets of lodgings of the dead man being linked to yourself, makes it relevant. So Wiltons was your only foray into the theatrical world. Did you leave Wiltons because you were getting married?"

"No Inspector. The two were not connected. I left Wiltons because I was not suited to the music hall life, neither as a performer or personally. I had hoped to find an opening in the legitimate theatre, but was unsuccessful but fortunately, I then met my husband and married."

"I see. Is this the only address you have lived at since your marriage, Mrs Brunswick?"

"No. At first, we had a small apartment in Victoria Street but that was not suitable so my husband acquired the lease of this house."

"Well thank you, madam. Perhaps you will be good enough to ask your husband to come to the station this evening as soon as it is convenient."

"To what end, Inspector?"

"To answer some questions, madam."

Brannan got up and made it clear that was the end of the interview but as he made to leave he said, almost as an afterthought "But we may need to ask you to come to the station also at some time in the future."

60

Detective Sergeant Clarke arrived at the Borough Road police station in the middle of the afternoon. The Inspector was in and the sergeant immediately told him the reason for the visit.

"It appears that your Mr Partner is not in any way connected with the special political branch of the Dublin police and he is not connected with us at Scotland Yard."

"So what do you surmise from that?"

"Well sir, my contacts in Dublin suggest a possible set of circumstances., Guesswork of course. But feasible in my view. You may be aware there are a number of Fenian factions in different parts of Ireland, all mutually exclusive and no one group trusting another. They all have the same motivation, setting up a rebellion in Ireland and all raise funds for the purchase of arms. Some get money from the Irish Brotherhood in America, others carry out robberies and then there are forged banknotes and other criminal means. It is suggested that perhaps one of the groups not connected with the men who have the London bank accounts, got wind of them and decided to check up on how much money they had and where it came from."

"Well, Sergeant. You are much more cognisant of this kind of activity than I, so I must accept your word that it is feasible. Would you suggest then that there is no connection with this bank enquiry by Fenians and forged coins?"

"Well sir, If there was a connection between this Partner and your dead man then we cannot rule it out. If there was no connection then it seems unlikely. We have not come across anything like this before with the Fenians. That is not to say that it could not happen in the future. But the way in which they operate in small groups means that it would be more difficult for them to set up such an activity here in London. The same goes for the Russians."

"The Russians? What have they got to do with it?"

"Russian emigres are also mentioned in some circles as being a possible source of these coins as a means of funding insurrection back in Russia. I know no more than that, Inspector, but it seems unlikely to me."

"I agree with you there, Sergeant. We have some Irish here in the Borough, mostly labourers and unlikely to be Fenians and we have even fewer recognisable Russians."

The Sergeant grinned. "They don't all wear cloaks and carry bombs, Sir"

The Inspector acknowledge the riposte. "Thanks for coming over Sergeant. I can't say it has been a help in connection with the murder itself, but it has perhaps cleared away some debris. And if there is no real connection between the landlord and this Partner then it indicates that perhaps there was a connection with the lodger which needs further investigation."

The detective took his departure and Brannan returned to his own thoughts about his next move on the murder enquiry.

61

Brunswick had obviously come straight from his supper in Admiral Square as he arrived at the Borough Police Office at six thirty that evening.

"Inspector, I must say that I object most strongly to being summoned to attend here in this most peremptory manner."

"I am sorry, Mr Brunswick if your wife gave you that impression. You were not summoned here, if you had been I would have sent two constables and a police van for you. I asked your wife to ask you to come, and you have."

"My wife told me what you said and in my view, that was a summons."

"Obviously a misinterpretation, Mr Brunswick. Can we now turn to why you are here?"

"Yes of course"

"Why did you lie about your relationship with Mr Partner?"

"I do not understand."

"What is it about that question that you do not understand, Mr Brunswick? It was quite straightforward. Why did you lie?"

"And why do you say that I lied?"

"Mr Brunswick. At this rate, we are going to be here all night and I am sure that you would not wish to spend it in a police cell. This is a murder enquiry and it behoves you to be completely honest with your answers if you are to escape suspicion., So please do not prevaricate any further. Why did you lie?"

"I presume I am not under arrest and can leave at any moment?"

"You are not under arrest, Mr Brunswick, but you cannot leave until I say so. At the moment you are a witness. If you attempt to leave without answering honestly, the question I have put to you, then I will regard you as a suspect and hold you accordingly."

"Why should I be a suspect?"

"I cannot say this any differently than I have been for the last ten minutes, Mr Brunswick. Because you have lied to a police officer investigating a murder in which you are implicated."

"Why am I implicated?"

"For goodness sake man, why can't you see the position you are in and come clean? The murdered man lived at your house and you lied about your relationship to him."

"My only relationship with the man was that he lodged at my house."

"And how did he come to lodge at your house?"

"Mr Partner"

"Stop there Mr Brunswick if you are going to repeat the story about a recommendation from a business colleague. You hardly knew Partner so why would you accept a recommendation from him?"

"Admittedly I did not know him all that well, but I had some conversations with him and the subject came up. I said I needed a lodger and he said that he knew someone suitable."

"Just like that? Were you so desperate to have a lodger that you took on someone you did not know on the recommendation of another person you did not really know and made no enquiries about this prospective lodger?"

"If you put it like that. Yes"

"Why so desperate, then Mr Brunswick?"

"I do not think that is any of your business."

"As I have already pointed out, this is a murder enquiry. Everything related to the dead man is relevant and therefore our business. We need to know how it was and under what circumstances this stranger came to live under your roof. We need to know that in order to understand how it was that he was later found dead not a stone's throw from your house and you did not know he was missing"

"We did not think he was missing. He was away on one of his business trips."

"That's as maybe. Now back to Mr Partner. How many times did you actually meet him in the short time that he was at the bank?"

"Perhaps three or four"

"And on those three or four occasions you built up such a rapport that you discussed your private financial affairs and told him you were hard up, could not really afford the expensive lease you had undertaken as well as a new wife and he commiserated with you?"

"Now you are being offensive Inspector and you have no right."

"Not at all Mr Brunswick. Merely attempting to fill in the blanks which you leave in your account of your relationship with this stranger."

"I told you, he was not a stranger and I trusted his judgement."

"But in any normal usage of the word, Mr Brunswick. he was a stranger. You had met him three or four times only. You had probably had more conversations with the news-vendor standing outside your bank than you had with Partner"

"Perhaps so. But he was an accountant like myself so as I said, I trusted his judgement."

"During your conversations with Partner, did he tell you for whom he was working?"

"Not at that time no. He mentioned a firm in the city that he had worked for previously. I had dealings with them a few years ago and we discussed mutual acquaintances there, so I knew that his claim was genuine."

"But not who he was working for at that time?"

"I assumed it was the Irish bank that gave him the letter of introduction."

"Would that necessarily have been the case?"

"No. These audits are often carried out on behalf of third parties."

"During your discussions with Partner, apart from your private affairs, did you discuss the accounts he was auditing?"

"No. That would have been unprofessional. There must be no suggestion of any undue influences being brought to bear on how an audit is conducted."

"So you say that the story you told of Sylvester being recommended by Partner is true except for exaggerating his role at the bank and how you came to know him."

"I suppose if you put it like that, yes."

"But no lie as such?"

"I did not lie."

"But you did not take the normal precautions that a man of your profession would have been expected to make."

"That is not a criminal offence."

"No it is not. But when you obfuscate about it during a murder enquiry then it will look suspicious and unlikely, Professional financial experts would normally be expected to carry their expertise into their private lives. You do not appear to have done that. This man that you took into your home turns out to be a possible criminal and ends up with a violent death. This shows that your judgement was at fault and there must have been a very serious reason for that."

"I reject your reasoning, Inspector."

"Perhaps so. Mr Brunswick, but it is reasoning and what you are asking me to believe is not reasonable. If you persist in what you say, then I must regard your answers as being unsatisfactory and therefore suspect. In those circumstances, I will need to have enquiries made about your private life and financial circumstances. Those enquiries will no doubt get to the ears of your employers."

"Are you threatening me? Inspector."

"Not at all Mr Brunswick. This is a simple statement of fact. As a witness, your answers have not been satisfactory and I would be failing in my duty if I did not enquire into the reasons for that. If you have nothing further to add, then you may go."

Brunswick rose from his chair but the Inspector continued without looking up from the notes he was making on the yellow pad in front of him

"But I would urge you to think about what I have said. If you have any information at all about this lodger which you have not divulged then please feel free to come back and see me at any time."

Brunswick resumed his seat.

"Very well Inspector I will explain my reasons to you. But in private."

Brannan nodded to the constable who left the room.

"Do you wish to make a statement? If so I will call the constable back and he will take it down for you. Or do you just want to tell me why you lied.?"

"I must repeat that I did not lie, Inspector."

"Well we shall see. Please proceed, Mr Brunswick."

"Where shall I start?"

"You are the one who said that you had something to tell me. So you decide. Perhaps with the true story about your relationship with Sylvester."

"There was no relationship Inspector. He answered an advertisement I placed in the evening paper for a lodger.

"You advertised"

"Yes. The cost of our married lifestyle was more than my salary was able to bear, and my savings are virtually exhausted."

"Would you like to explain."

"Prior to my marriage, I lived in a small but comfortable apartment in Victoria. It was a reasonable rent and it suited me and I could live well within my means and acquired some savings.

The apartment was not to my wife's liking so we eventually acquired the lease of the house in Admiral Square, even though it was really more than I could afford and was larger than was necessary for the two of us."

"Presumably though the size was with the intention of starting a family?"

"Yes of course, that was a consideration, although not put into so many words."

"But you are an accountant, surely you did your sums before embarking on an expenditure you could not afford"

"Of course I calculated that I could afford the house, but we had not been married all that long and I failed to factor in the full cost of maintaining a wife. I did not know that my wife was not accustomed to living economically."

"She has expensive tastes?"

"You could put it like that"

"So when the bills started to come in you found you could not pay them. Not a good reputation for the accountant at a bank."

"Precisely."

"So you decided to take in a lodger. How did that come about?"

"I discussed the matter with my wife and rather than have stringent restrictions placed on her spending she agreed to have a lodger."

"Did you discuss how you would acquire a lodger?"

"Yes. I knew she would not approve of advertising so I intended to make enquiries among acquaintances. However no one that I knew needed lodgings and I did not wish to give the impression that I was in financial difficulties. Mr Sylvester replied to the advertisement and when I had interviewed him, I told my wife he had been recommended by a colleague."

"You then went through a charade of reinterviewing him again at home."

"Yes"

"But how did you satisfy yourself about his suitability?"

"He gave me references from previous landlords which I accepted at face value."

"You did not check them?"

"No. And as it turned out for two months all went well so during that time I had no reason to doubt his suitability. He was quiet when in the house and came and went as he said that he would. Away for several days at a time and then returning. He did not require any cleaning, meals or laundry, so in every way an ideal tenant."

"Except that he was not who he said he was."

"I did not know that."

"No, but you would have if you had checked his references. You would then have found that he had used at least two different names at previous addresses."

"Well with hindsight, I agree."

"So then when he turned up dead as it were, you decided that you had to tell the police the same story as you had told your wife. As a result of that deception, we have spent considerable time and expense in chasing after your Mr Partner."

"But I was not to know that."

"No, you would not have been able to know that. But you did know that the dead man was your lodger and failed to recognise him. Why was that?"

"Because I did not recognise him. I have not seen many dead bodies and he looked different laying there in the mortuary."

"Well maybe. We will leave it at that for the time being Mr Brunswick. I will need to speak to you again in the coming days and you can advise your wife that I will be calling to see her also. "

"Will you need to tell her what I have said about Partner and the reasons for it?"

"Not necessarily, but it will be a judgement I will have to make at the time."

62

Brunswick returned to his anxious wife. "Well James, what did he have to say?"

"Rose, he just wanted to go over how Sylvester came to be here"

"But why keep on asking? Are we under suspicion?"

"Why should we be? He was a lodger and that was all we need to tell them. He was not a friend and we have not known him long enough to make him an enemy. Whey then should they consider that we would have any motive for killing him?"

"I am sure that they do. That Inspector is a rough sort of character and I would not put it past him to try to implicate us for no reason than that he has no one else to consider. And that constable always looks as though he is trying to guess what we are hiding."

"I have told you. There is no reason for them to think that we are hiding anything. As you say, it would appear that they have no suspects, so they are looking at us for no other reason."

"I am still worried, James. Is there nothing we can do to make them look elsewhere?"

"Laying a false trail do you mean?

"Well I had not thought of it like that. But perhaps yes. An imitation fox trail is often used in the training of hounds so perhaps our detectives could learn something by being sent off on a wild goose chase."

"I am not sure how that could be contrived. And if it was discovered that it was a deliberate false trail and it led back to us, we would be in worse straits than we are now."

"Perhaps you are right James. But it irks me that we can do nothing whilst they ferret around in our private lives."

"Well we shall have to wait and see. The Inspector said that he would need to come and see you again, so you will have to be very careful what you say. There is no point in getting angry about the questions and thus giving an answer which provides them with ammunition for more questions."

"I know what you mean James. But I am not a fool and will do my best to guard my tongue. But I do get annoyed by the attitude that they can say and do whatever they like just because they are policemen."

63

George spent the afternoon in Admiral square, but did not visit the fair Alice.

He was fortunate in catching the Brunswicks' cook, Maud Wright, as she came round the corner into the square. Although she claimed to be too busy to stop and talk George assured her that it would be brief and was important. Had anything different happened in the house when the lodger went missing? She told him that there had been, perhaps, a strange incident when she was sent home early on the day of the storm. A Wednesday. Maud had accepted this act of generosity from her employer in view of the bad weather. However, although Mrs Brunswick said she would serve the prepared meal herself it had not been eaten. The cook had made no comment to Mrs Brunswick about this the following day but had served up a different meal.

Mrs Wright fortunately knew where Sally the Brunswick's maid at the time had her new position and it was not far away.

It was necessary to follow the middle-class protocol of asking her new employers for permission to speak to her. It was given and Sally just repeated what she had told him previously. But George pressed her to think about anything which had occurred in the house on the week of the murder that was different. She struggled with that. Was not sure about the days of the week even. Then she brightened and said, "Well there was the rug."

"The rug?"

"A fireside rug in the sitting room."

"What about it?"

"It was a green one, but it wasn't there one morning. A different one was there which didn't really fit. I asked Mrs Brunswick about it and she said she didn't like the first one any more so had changed it. Put it in another room. She didnt usually do any work in the house and I didn't see the green rug in any other room."

"Why did you leave the Brunswicks Sally? Did they dismiss you or did you find this new position first?"

"She just said one day they didnt need me any more. It was the day after you had come. But it was lucky really cos I got this new place right away and its full time and I am happy here."

George thanked the girl and her employer who had been hovering in the background all this time and left. He hoped that he had not placed Sally's new job in jeopardy by his visit, but it was necessary.

Should he go to find that rug at number forty-two? He had no warrant and could not demand anything. If the Brunswicks were involved in the death of their lodger, as it now appears, then there had been plenty of time to destroy any evidence as well as dismissing the maid. Forgetting about the carpet bag in the wardrobe had been an oversight but there was not guarantee that they had other mistakes. Up until now the pair had managed to fend off any real suggestion that they were involved in the man's death.

64

The Inspector had decided on a plan of action for the continuation of the investigation which was confirmed when Morrison reported back with his findings from his interviews with the cook and the maid.

There were now no other suspects although the motive was still not clear.

He addressed this concern to Morrison who sat opposite him in the office

"If we look at the Brunswicks as possibly the perpetrators of this crime, Sir, then they could have several possible motives."

"Go on."

"First Mr Brunswick. Sexual jealousy if he discovered the his wife and the lodger were having an affair."

Brannan groaned. "I am not asking you for more fictional fantasy Morrison."

"You did ask for possible motives, Sir, I was just going to enumerate possibilities of which I believe there are several."

"Go on then, but try to stick to feasible ones."

"I will try, Sir, but I still consider that what I suggested is within the bounds of possibility. Mrs Brunswick is alone in the house for much of the week apart from part-time staff. They do not appear to have any social life and Mrs Brunswick was attracted to the idea of being on the stage. Therefore, I consider that perhaps she was not attracted to the domestic life she found in Admiral Square. We know that Da Sylva or Sylvester was prone to approach women for sex. If Mrs Brunswick responded to his advances out of boredom or whatever, and her husband discovered this then we have a motive for the murder of the paramour.

Another possibility is that the lodger approached his landlady and was rejected. She told her husband who ordered the lodger to leave forthwith and violence ensued ending in the death of the lodger."

The Inspector liked the second suggestion better than the first, but it was still conjecture.

"Well then sir, if we take Mrs Brunswick as the possible killer. The lodger approaches her, she repulses him and he tries to force her. A struggle ensues, there are fire-irons in the grate and she picks up a poker to defend herself.

Continuing with Mrs Brunswick, we do not know if the husband was aware of her appearances at the music hall whereas it is feasible that the lodger did. A chance of blackmail and once again violence could ensue."

"Any more? Morrison."

"Without continuing with more speculation about motive, Sir, there is no doubt about the circumstantial evidence. The carpet bag still being in the room when it should not have been, and the fireside rug being moved by a woman who never did housework and the cook being sent home early on the day we think the man died."

The Inspector did not respond immediately.

"I will grant you the circumstantial evidence, but by itself it is a bit thin and even if a magistrate accepted them, I doubt if a Bailey jury would. We are going to need some hard evidence or a confession."

"It is a bit late for hard evidence being discovered at the house, Inspector. There has been too much time to get rid of it. The carpet bag was overlooked but since then there would have been time to clear everything up. If the Brunswicks are involved then it has to be the two of them as it is not feasible for either to have done it alone. They got rid of the maid and the cook only ever came upstairs to set up and serve the meal."

"I am not going to argue with the logic of what you have said, Morrison, and I commend you for the thought that you have put into this case. But perhaps it is a mistake to take all these small instances to build a case against a middle-class couple when dealing with the death of a man with criminal connections. We cant lose sight of his background and his involvement in forged coins. That kind of criminality does not usually involve violence, but this is a case where potentially large sums of money are involved. Large sums of money frequently result in violence."

"I agree, Sir. But we have not turned up any potential suspects in that side of the equation. If violence was going to ensue as a result of his coining involvement, why wait until he is here in the Borough? Why not kill him in Stepney or Birmingham? If east end criminals are involved in his death then surely they would have preferred their home ground where in fact his body could have been disposed of never to be found. If the murder was premeditated I would have thought he would have been lured back to the other side of the river, which would not have been difficult if he was offered a substantial incentive."

There was really no arguing with this logic but the inspector still demurred.

"But a criminal's death is much more likely to be at the hands of a criminal than a banker and his wife. I don't like those two any more than you do, but we must not let any prejudice on that score stop us thinking clearly about what evidence we have."

"If that is true, Inspector. Then we have nothing to go on. There was no evidence in the watchhouse that the murder had taken place there, in fact the opposite. Everything pointed to the body having been placed there after death. No sign of a struggle and very little blood. The only evidence we have of his criminal involvement lay on the other side of the river not here in the Borough. We have found no one that knew him here except where he lodged. Our enquiries among those suspected of coining in this division found no one admitting knowing him or having been approached by him. If his connection with the coins was to try to wholesale them, then he had ample time to put out feelers on this side of the river. We found no mention of that in the division."

65

Brannan decided to continue with the softly softly approach as Brunswick sat opposite him in his office.

"I am sure, Mr Brunswick that you are fully aware as to why you and your wife have been brought here."

"No, I am not. It was unseemly to be brought here in your police van and I will take the earliest opportunity of making a complaint to the commissioner. We are not just common criminals, you know, to be treated like this."

"I accept that you are not common criminals, Mr. Brunswick but there is not much doubt that you are criminals. Even if you did not kill your lodger then you know who did and have concealed that fact. That in its self is a crime."

"Do you have any evidence at all to support that assertion?"

"We have plenty of evidence to support that assertion Mr Brunswick. The man was clearly killed on your premises from a blow to the head. His body was then conveyed from your house to the churchyard of St. Mary Magdalen. Since that time you have denied all knowledge of those events even though they could not have taken place without your cognisance."

Brunswick continued to resist. "But what evidence do you have to support this bizarre story?"

"Sufficient evidence to take you before a magistrate and have you charged."

"On a charge of murder?"

"Not necessarily. We may charge your wife instead with that crime."

"Has my wife admitted this offence?"

"Of course not. I have not spoken to her yet. Perhaps she will admit to the crime herself or tell us that you delivered the fatal blow. I was going to give you another opportunity to tell the truth about what happened on that night."

"I have nothing more to say on the subject and I demand to be present when you speak to my wife."

Brannan sighed. "Mr Brunswick, it is clear that you have not yet understood the gravity of your situation. You are in no position to demand anything. I will speak to your wife and, if appropriate, I will tell you what she says."

Both Sergeant Brewer and Morrison had stood silently at the back of the room for the whole time of the interview.

Morrison had been taking notes of what had taken place in his own version of shorthand.

The Inspector stood Up. "If you have nothing further to say Mr Brunswick then I will see what your wife has to say for herself. At the moment it appears that you will both be remaining at this station until the morning."

Brunswick began to protest then appeared to think better of it, perhaps deciding to await events.

Morrison left the room to get Mrs Brunswick from the small anteroom where she waited.

Brewer escorted Brunswick from the office and the couple passed each other in the corridor but did not speak.

66

The Inspector had decided to get straight to the point. "I am going to be frank with you Mrs Brunswick" he began "and must tell you that both you and your husband are in a parlous position."

The woman did not respond. Sitting impassively across the desk from the inspector it was clear to him that she intended to be even more stubborn that she had been when he had spoken to her at home.

He wondered about her background that gave her this poise in a very difficult situation. Most young women of her age would be almost prostrate with anxiety, and here she was just sitting there. Had she perhaps had more training in the dramatic arts than she had revealed previously. Was this all just an act?

"Tell me about your life, before the music hall, Mrs Brunswick."

That threw her and she did not respond for a couple of minutes.

"I cannot see what that has to do with why I am here."

"All will be revealed Mrs Brunswick. You are likely to be appearing in the magistrates court on Monday morning either alone or jointly with your husband. Now please tell me how you lived before the music hall and marrying you husband."

She still resisted. "What charges do you intend to bring against us."

"As I have said. All will be revealed and how you answer my questions now may well influence the severity of the charges to be laid."

"I do not understand."

"Please tell me about yourself Mrs Brunswick and then we can move on. For instance, what is your maiden name?"

"I was born Mary Dickinson in Hemel Hempstead, my father was the vicar of that parish. I had private schooling and excelling at singing and drama decided to try my hand at appearing on the stage. My father did not approve of course so I chose a stage name. I soon found that the music hall did not suit me. I had no success at appearing in the legitimate theatre, met James at the house of a mutual friend and we later married."

At last some background on this woman. So she had excelled at drama. Was she still excelling? Was everything a performance for her? So let's go along with this. If she is acting then perhaps a little drama in the opposite direction may not come amiss

"Mrs Brunswick, how soon after your lodger came to the house did he make his first advances to you?"

"He did not make any advances to me."

"I find that difficult to believe. He was a known womaniser. You are an attractive woman alone in the house from time to time so he would not have been able to resist."

"If he made advances, then I did not recognise them as such and therefore would not have responded."

"Did he ever mention that he had seen you performing at Wiltons?"

"No"

Morrison was certain that the woman was lying but relying on the fact that the lodger was dead, so you could deny with impunity whatever had taken place Bertelsen them. Brannan had come to the same conclusion.

"Mrs Brunswick it is clear you do not intend to cooperate. So you will remain here until Monday morning when you will be taken before a magistrate.

"But you have not said what you intend to charge me with. You have not even said why we are here."

"Perhaps I had assumed that you would know why you are here. Your lodger died in your house from a blow to the head. His body was carted to the churchyard and dumped in the watchhouse. The coroner has decided that he was murdered so therefore you will be charged with his murder or with complicity in it."

"That is ridiculous. You have no evidence that he died in the house let alone was murdered there."

"All the evidence that we do have points to that conclusion and is sufficient to have you arraigned. As we do not know who struck the fatal blow then you will be equally charged. You of course cannot be compelled to give evidence against your husband, but there is nothing to stop him giving evidence against you."

She remained silent so that after a couple of minutes the Inspector was forced to resume.

"It is surprising that you appear to be so unconcerned about the possibility of an Old Bailey trial resulting in your being hanged, Mrs Brunswick."

The former actress continued to remain silent. Brannan was now convinced that this situation had been carefully rehearsed. Of course, she could not have known that all the facts would point to them. But somehow she had prepared herself for being confronted and was consummately ready. But he had plenty of time and could possibly wear her down.

"Very well then. Constable take Mrs Brunswick to a cell and bring her husband here."

She broker silence then. "Am I to take it that I am now a prisoner, Inspector?"

"Unless you can give me some evidence that you were not involved in the death of your lodger, then yes you are a prisoner and will be brought before the magistrate on Monday morning. In the meantime you will remain at this station, I will speak again with your husband and if he can convince me of his innocence then he can go home but otherwise, he also will remain."

"But surely I am entitled to be told what you are charging me with."

"You have been told. You will be charged with being involved in the unlawful killing of your lodger. The magistrate can decide on what specific charge he will send with you to the central criminal court."

Morrison was still standing by, expecting some outburst from the woman, but none came. She retained her almost impassivity and stood until the constable opened the door and she went towards it. There was still time for her to change her mind about making a statement, but she did not take the opportunity.

67

Morrison returned to the Inspector's office without Brunswick.

"Where is the man?" the Inspector growled. He was getting tired and irritated and Morrison wondered if he had been wise in risking this just to share a thought.

"Sir, I realise that you may well have spotted this but I thought I should mention it just in case."

"What do you think you should mention in case I had missed it?"

Getting worse.

"Well, sir. I had noticed that both the Brunswicks have been very careful in the language that they used, almost as if it had been rehearsed."

"Yes. I had noticed that the woman was demonstrating her dramatic skills here. The thought of rehearsed responses had also crossed my mind. But what about the man?"

"Well sir, she appears to be the stronger of the two."

"I had not noticed that. What makes you say it."

"I have little experience of women sir, as you know. But behind this young woman from a small country town, there is a strong personality. I am from a small village myself and learned from an early age that women can have many faces. Some can be pious in church but positive viragos when slighted or protecting their children."

"Well that may be the case, but it is not relevant to what you were suggesting about their statements."

"Sir, its just that they both seem to be emphasising that either there had been no murder or that if there had, it was not them. They are not denying in so many words that they were not involved in the death. They are both saying that we have no evidence that the death occurred at the house. But that is not the same as saying that it did not. Almost as if they were preparing to later claim that there had been some kind of accident. It all seems so prepared with similar language which implies that whatever happened, they were both involved"

"Well I agree with that and you are right to draw my attention to it. So let's have him back in."

"One other thing sir, if I may. We still do not know if he was aware that his wife had been a music hall performer. It may be relevant."

"I did not ask her that. Perhaps I should have done. No matter we will ask him."

Brunswick was certainly not as calm as his wife. "Inspector this is intolerable. You have no reason to assume that we were involved in the death of Sylvester and you certainly have no evidence that he died in our house. I think that I should be allowed to consult a lawyer."

"Well Mr Brunswick, there is no doubt that you are going to require the services of a lawyer and indeed a barrister when you appear at the Old Bailey. In the meantime ,you can continue to answer my questions."

"I have already told you everything that I know about the man. I was not involved in his death and I do not know how he came by his injuries."

"I am prepared to accept that statement from you Mr Brunswick, but will you be willing to swear under oath that you were not involved in attempting to dispose of his body?"

"As far as I am concerned, Inspector I will never be in the position of having to swear under oath about anything relating to this matter."

"You amaze me, Mr Brunswick, how you manage to dance around and prevaricate to avoid answering direct questions. Did you study law, perhaps before taking up accountancy?"

Brunswick chose to ignore the question. "So when can I see a lawyer?"

"When you have answered all of my questions Mr Brunswick and after you appear before the magistrate. You will then have plenty of time to consult a lawyer whilst waiting at Newgate to appear at the Central criminal court."

"You have decided to charge me then?"

"I told you that before."

"I will answer no more questions then"

"You can remain silent if you wish. But if you are going to plead ignorance then all the evidence will lead to your wife acting alone in this matter, which many juries will find difficult to accept."

"You have no more evidence against my wife than you have against me."

"There is evidence enough, Mr Brunswick. You are right that we do not have witnesses to the actual injury but there is sufficient other evidence to show that it was caused at your house and the body removed from there."

"That is preposterous and you know it."

"Not at all if you care to think about it instead of blustering. For instance, you claim that the dead man answered an advertisement in order to become your lodger. How many replies did you receive to that advertisement?"

"Just the one."

"Was that not strange?"

"I do not know. I had never advertised before, so did not know what to expect."

"And when you saw this solitary responder for the first time did he indicate why he had chosen to answer your advertisement?"

"He said he was not happy living in the east end having come from Birmingham and wanted somewhere better. I tested his financial situation by asking for a quarters rent in advance to which he agreed."

"So the money was the deciding factor. As long as he could pay you were not concerned with his probity."

"He appeared respectable and said he was a professional metallurgist."

"He could have claimed to be a magician as far as you were concerned as long as he could pay. Did you and your wife discuss this before you took him into your home?"

"No."

"So when did you discover that he was not as respectable as you supposed him to be?"

"I do not understand. What do you mean."

"Well at some stage he made advances to your wife whilst your were out."

"She did not tell me about that."

"Why do you think that was?"

"I am not sure."

"So when did you become aware of it without your wife telling you?"

"I did not become aware of it and as far as I know it did not happen."

"So when did you discover that Sylvester had seen your wife performing at Wiltons music hall?"

"I did not know that he had seen her."

"But you know now. That much is clear. Were you aware that your wife was or had been a music hall performer when you married?"

"No, she did not tell me that."

"If she had, would that have made a difference in your proposal of marriage?"

"No. I have no prejudice in that direction."

"So when did you learn that she had appeared at Wiltons Music Hall?

"I am not sure."

"Mr Brunswick. What you say goes beyond the bounds of possibility. You discover, or are told that your wife of barely a year had been a music hall performer prior to your marriage and you do not recall when or how you came by that information."

"No. I cant be certain."

"So was it before or after the lodger?"

"Is this relevant to anything at all, Inspector. You claim to be seeking information about the death of Mr. Sylvester, but continue to ask about things that are none of your business."

"I should not need to remind you that this is a murder investigation Mr Brunswick. Everything is relevant until it can be discounted."

" I have told you I do not remember."

"Yes, you have. And I do not believe you because it is unbelievable. So do you wish to have some time to reconsider what you have told me before or are you now prepared to tell the truth?"

"I have told you the truth."

"No, Mr Brunswick, You have replied to my questions with carefully worded responses which have not revealed what you know about the death of this man."

"I have told you the truth. I was not involved with the death of this man."

"But you were involved in the disposal of the body in a callous and disreputable manner."

Brunswick did not reply.

Brannan waited.

"Do you deny what I have just said."

"I do not think that I need to deny what is pure conjecture."

"Well, it is clear that you intend to be obdurate in this. I will advise you, however, that it will not serve you well in the magistrates' court on Monday morning. If you refuse to speak in answer to the charges, the magistrate will have no option but to send you for trial. That is how it works. You will remain here this evening and will be given another opportunity to speak in the morning."

There was still no response from the man.

"Constable take the prisoner to the desk and enter the charge on which he is being held as being involved in the unlawful killing of Da Silva otherwise known as Sylvester. Then bring Mrs Brunswick here."

"You cant do that" Brunswick protested, "You have no evidence."

"Mr Brunswick I have no intention, at this hour, of going over all that again. I will see you in the morning."

Morrison approached the man and ostentatiously produced his handcuffs. They were not necessary. Brunswick rose and indicated that he would go with the constable.

69

Mrs Brunswick walked into the room ahead of Morrison and sat on the chair opposite the inspector without being invited to do so.

"I have nothing further to say, Inspector."

"I had no intention of asking you any further questions, Madam, I called you in to advise you formally that you are to be charged with being involved in the unlawful killing of your lodger. You will be held here overnight. Tomorrow you will be given an opportunity to make a statement in answer to that charge. On Monday morning you will be taken before a magistrate who will decide what to do with you."

She did not respond. Brannan was grateful for that he was tired of these two and their fencing. There was no doubt of their guilt in his mind and he would be glad to leave it to the magistrate on Monday.

"Constable take the prisoner and charge her. Then take her to the cells and ensure that there is no communication between the two of them."

Morrison returned to the Inspector's office with a grin on his face.

Brannan saw the look and just raised his eyebrows.

"Sir. Here is a bunch of keys in the possession of the male prisoner and here is the old padlock from the watchhouse. One of the keys opens this padlock."

"A fairly common type of padlock. One of these keys would probably open the padlocks we use at the station."

"No sir. this is an old design. None of these keys will open our padlocks. I have tried."

"Still not evidence, Morrison."

"No, Sir. Not by itself. But it is physical evidence which we have not had before which links Mr. Brunswick to the watchhouse. It should help the magistrate to agree a referral to the central criminal court. Shall I bring Brunswick back in?"

"Good Lord no, Morrison. You must be as tired of these two as I am. Leave them untill the morning. I have said they will be given a chance to make statements. Perhaps the key and the padlock will open one of their lips."

72

Brunswick showed signs of having slept in his clothes in the cell, but was still belligerent and prepared to continue with his previous attitude to the questioning.

"Mr Brunswick. You know what you are going to be charged with at the magistrates' court tomorrow. Have you decided what answer to make to the charges?"

"I shall deny the charges, obviously."

"Despite the evidence?"

"You have no evidence."

"Perhaps you would care to explain why a key in your possession was used to unlock the padlock at the watchhouse where your lodger's body was found."

"I cannot explain that and I do no see why I have to. How can you possibly know that key was used in the way you suggested."

"Because there are marks on the key, which correspond to some on the padlock itself. But how then do you explain that the bassinet originally in an outhouse at your address was found adjacent to that same watchhouse?"

"I am sure that a mark on a key is not evidence. And how do you know that the bassinet you found is the same one that was at our house?"

"Because we have a witness who was aware of a specific mark on the bassinet at your house which is also on the bassinet discovered near the watchhouse."

"Another mark or scratch no doubt." he sneered.

"All evidence adding up, Mr Brunswick. Are you sure that you do not want to tell me what really happened to your lodger?"

"I have told you before I had no involvement in the death of the man."

"So you have said. But you have not said that you were not involved in the disposal of the body."

"If I was not involved in the death then it follows that I was not involved in the disposal of the body, as you put it."

"I doubt that a magistrate or a jury, for that matter, would agree with you. Particularly in view of the fact that you are an admitted liar, who is going to believe anything that you say."

"I am a respectable man employed at a merchant bank and will rely on that to prove my veracity."

"But you have already disproved your veracity here in this police office in front of witnesses. You lied about your original connection with the lodger with a complete fabrication. You are clearly skilled in telling stories. I wonder what we would unearth about your background if we went into in any great detail. As you admit to being in sufficient financial difficulties to necessitate taking in a lodger, I wonder what your employers would find if they had a good look at any possible irregularities at the bank."

"They would find nothing."

"Because there is nothing to find, or because you have been good at covering your tracks?"

"The former. I have not touched a penny at the bank. You are being too clever, Inspector. If I had stolen money from the bank then I would not be in financial difficulties."

"You may not have been able to steal sufficient to satisfy the needs of an expensive wife, Mr. Brunswick. That does not mean that you did not steal any at all. You are prepared to lie so it will not be difficult for anyone to believe that you are also prepared to steal. And perhaps commit murder."

"I have not stolen anything and I have not murdered anyone."

"But you have disposed of the body of a murdered man, of that, I am convinced and it is unlikely that any jury would come to a different conclusion."

70

On his way from his digs to the station he walked along Snowsfields and glancing down Melior Street he noticed a bassinet standing outside one of the houses. It was a fine morning so that it was not usual for babies to be outside in the relative fresh air.

But bassinets or perambulators were not common in that part of Bermondsey so his curiosity aroused and not having a firm time to attend the station, he diverted.

The pram stood outside the house of a woman that he had spoken to in the past who was not as suspicions of the police as many others. There was a baby in the pram and the front door was open.

He called "Mrs Wales are you there?"

"Corse I'm ere. what would you think? Oh, it's you Constable Morrison. What's the problem?

"No problem as far as I am aware Mrs Wales. Just curious about your new perambulator."

"What about it?"

"It looks quite new and although being a single man I know nothing about the price of these items I can imagine it would be quite expensive."

"What you suggestin'. We nicked it?"

"Not suggesting anything. But I would be interested in where it came from."

"My brother Fred found it in an alley orf Long Lane with buckled wheels so brought it round to me and my Alf fixed it up. Aint nicked if it was frown away."

"That's as may be Mrs Wales. I will make a few enquiries about it so don't get rid of it until I speak to you again."

"Why would I get rid? It's handy for the baby and the others as well."

"OK. Thanks for telling me about it."

She sniffed and turned her back. *Oh well, that's the end of one of the few friendly faces in this street.*

Fortunately, the inspector was in his office when Morrison arrived at the station so he was able to add this bit of information.

"Sir you will recall that you considered that if the murder took place in Admiral Square then how did T the body get to the watchhouse without it being observed. This morning I discovered that a fairly new perambulator was found abandoned nearby a couple of weeks ago."

"A perambulator to carry a full grown man? I think you are off into fiction again Morrison and the sooner you are back on the beat the better."

George half expected this response but thought that one more try to justify himself could not do any harm.

"This perambulator is fairly new and of an expensive kind, Sir, as far as I am able to judge. In normal circumstances, it would have stood out in the back streets of the Borough. I am told that the wheels were buckled almost beyond repair so that it had been used to carry a load in excess of that it was designed for."

"All right Morrison. Sit down and continue your speculation about the connection to this case and how it fits into our case against the Brunswicks."

"I have thought about it, Sir. The body would need to have been conveyed on some kind of wheeled vehicle with the intention of disposing of it. A handcart perhaps or a coster's barrow or cart. The Brunswicks would have no access to such and carrying the body through the streets was not practical. Some improvisation would be necessary. The only wheeled vehicle generally available in most households is a box on wheels for carrying coal and the like or a perambulator. The usual box on wheels is mostly too small to carry a body which leaves only a perambulator. If one was used but the wheels buckled near the watchhouse, then that could explain why it was there. If a perambulator was the means of carrying the body it could be a good disguise in the bad weather we have been experiencing. The dead man came from Stepney to the Borough and one of the inhabitants of Admiral Square also had previous connections with that part of London as we showed from your chart. What if we could show that they had another connection. Access or use of a perambulator."

The Inspector sat silently through this lengthy explanation of George's thought process. He admitted to himself that it was all logical but unlikely.

Morrison waited for further instructions. So off he went to Admiral Square to check for perambulators at number forty-two. He returned within half an hour with confirmation from the cook.

71

Mrs Brunswick was showing some signs of her night in the cell when when she was again brought to the inspectors office,

"Have you re4considered your decision to make a statement in connection with the death of your lodger, madam?"

She did not answer.

"The bassinet you owned Mrs Brunswick. Did that indicate that you are now pregnant?"

"It is most unseemly of you to ask a lady a question like that Inspector Brannan and I will report this to your superiors."

Brannan did not respond. Sometimes a pause could be useful and rarely wrong. If she was going to pursue the matter then he could not be in more trouble than he was now, but she might use the pause to reflect. He was right.

"I have never owned a bassinet, Inspector, so your question was not only improper but incorrect but I will let it pass."

"My question was not intended to be personal but there is or was a bassinet in your house at some time, because it was seen there. Naturally, I assumed that it belonged to you, as you have so few staff."

"The bassinet was there in an outhouse when we arrived and it is no longer there, so I assumed that it had been collected by the former occupants."

"Have you any idea when it went missing?"

"Inspector, I did not say it had gone missing but that it was no longer there and I do not know when it went."

"Thank you, Mrs Brunswick. I am sure the magistrate will take your background and your lack of knowledge about the disappearance of the bassinet and your claimed lack of knowledge of everything relating to the death of your lodger into consideration in his decision on Monday morning."

There was no response so Brannan indicated that Morrison should escort her out of the room.

73

Brannan had just finished writing up his notes when the Superintendent walked in.

"I see that you have decided to charge the people from Admiral Square, Inspector. I hope you have sufficient evidence. I see you are not actually charging them with murder, which presumably means you are unsure."

"Not at all, Sir. I am sure that one of them killed him and together they disposed of the body."

"But what about evidence?"

Brannan gave a resume of everything that they had against the couple.

His superior listened politely enough but still responded: "Not much firm evidence, though, is there?"

"Mostly circumstantial sir, I will admit, but should be sufficient for the magistrate and a good prosecutor at the Bailey would make the charge stick."

"Perhaps you are right and I hope so. We do not need an acquittal in this kind of case in this division. But this is not why I am here although related to your murder. Apparently the detective branch have been watching a small factory in Shadwell in connection with these coins. The Mint were not involved and only the Commissioner was aware of it and presumably the Home Office. Yesterday the detective branch and a squad of soldiers from the Tower prepared to raid the place, but before they could go in there was an explosion. It would appear the place was booby trapped. What remained inside made it clear that this was the machinery involved in this coin making."

"Were there any bodies inside?"

"No. None. It is clear that our famous detective branch is not as clever as they think they are. They must have been spotted and the forgers decided that they could not remove the machinery and decided to destroy it together with whatever evidence was in the building."

"Seems somewhat extreme."

"Perhaps, but we shall not know. I am told that the inside of the building was completely destroyed and that there is nothing of evidential value."

"I am not sure if this affects what we are doing here in connection with the murder. It shows that Da Silva's confederates are prepared to use extreme measures to cover their tracks, but it doesn't mean that they have used violence against our dead man here."

" I agree. I will report to the commissioner this morning and if he has any thoughts on the matter that will affect your going before the magistrate in the morning I will come back to you. In the meantime perhaps you should try to get some kind of admission from these two. If the connection with the forged coins is to be brought up in court then a clever defence lawyer could perhaps make something of it. Then he was gone.

74

Brannan mulled over the superintendent's visit for a while and then called Morrison back to his office. The constable had completed writing up his notes of the interviews with the Brunswicks and placed the substantial sheaf of papers on the inspectors desk.

The inspector told Morrison of the superintendents visit and his suggestion regarding an admission. The constable was doubtful. He thought that the inspector had pushed hard enough on the couple who seemed entrenched in the idea that there was not enough evidence against them. Only time and the courts would tell. The super was right of course. An admission would be better and certainly the possibility of the coining connection being used in the defence was clear.

"I am of the opinion, Inspector, that these two have little regard for the lower orders in the police service, but perhaps one last try with myself and another constable or perhaps Sergeant Brewer could go through the motions of taking a formal statement. We have not done this so far. Perhaps just ask them for a witness statement. They gave evidence at the inquest so they can hardly maintain this innocence approach and still refuse to give a formal statement."

"No that's not going to work Morrison. They have now been charged so we can hardly ask for a witness statement now. We should have thought of that tack before."

"Perhaps dangle the possibility of the charges being dropped if they give a statement?"

"No. No. Morrison. Can't do that. I am not against you interviewing them. Something could come of it and if they just clam up because you are a menial then we will have lost nothing. But then again another interview could give them the impression that we are desperate and make them even more intransigent."

"You are probably right sir. Have you prepared the case for the magistrate in the morning?"

"I think so, but I will just go through what you have brought me in case there is anything else that I can add. I cannot see that the magistrate will require a great deal to be convinced to refer them to the central criminal court and then the matter will be out of our hands. The commissioner's office will handle the rest."

"In view of the fact that this is not going to be an actual murder charge, Inspector, do you think that we should allow the lady to go home and have a change of clothes?"

"I hope you have not been smitten by this young woman, Morrison. We do not usually allow prisoners to go home and change their clothing."

"Far from being smitten, sir. I would not trust this one to tell the truth even in face of hellfire. But this is not a normal circumstance. The women who come in her usually arrive late at night and appear before the magistrate just as they are the following morning. The Brunswicks have been here since yesterday and are being kept until tomorrow, an unusually long time. It is difficult to second guess how she is going to react to any action on our part but a show of acceptance of the fact that she is a woman and may need facilities that we do not have, could be useful."

"Or the opposite."

"Exactly sir. But perhaps worth a try. She could be allowed to remain at home until tomorrow with a guard on the door or brought back here after she has changed her clothing. Whilst at the house we could take the opportunity of searching for the missing hearth rug and examining everything in that parlour which may have been used as a weapon"

"I will go along with that. Take Green with you and no doubt you will have at least half an hour in the parlour to have a search. If she doesn't want to walk to Admiral Square then offer the services of the police van."

75

The former music hall artiste had accepted the offer of being allowed to return home to change her clothes but declined to be conveyed in the police van.

When the three of them arrived at the house, Morrison reminded her that she was still a prisoner and would need to return to the station when she had completed her toilette. Her response was just a toss of the head.

As soon as she was safely upstairs he told Green to go to the outhouse and see if the missing hearthrug was secreted out there or anywhere on the outside of the house.

George went into the parlour and lifted up the new hearthrug that the maid had mentioned. There was no sign of any blood having seeped through onto the wood floor, but then that did not signify anything.

The cast iron fire surround was a fairly common design and the hearth protector had two horizontal bars and roundels at each end. The surround could not have been used as a weapon even though one of the roundels could have created the wound but Morrison examined it anyway. No sign of blood there either, but it had no doubt been black leaded several times since the death of the lodger.

Green returned and said that there was nothing in the outhouse except a few broken pieces of furniture.

Morrison went to have a look for himself. The broken furniture was a chair from the parlour and the break on the leg was new.

He brought it back into the parlour and the two constables continued their search of the room but nothing obviously related to the death could be found.

The woman returned to the parlour and made no comment, just stood their with her almost usual expression of disdain.

"Mrs Brunswick. Was this chair used to inflict the wound that killed your lodger?"

"Do not be ridiculous, constable. Even if it had I would not know. But that chair leg could not have inflicted such as wound as you put it."

"Why do you say that, madam?"

"Because the doctor went into great detail about that wound and described it as being caused by a rounded object."

"Something like the roundel on the edge of your hearth surround, perhaps."

"Possibly. But as I said I do not know. I was not here."

"But you saw the body. and you helped to clear up the evidence. What did you do with the hearthrug, Mrs Brunswick?" he pressed on, "Is it still hidden in the house? Under the stairs, perhaps?"

Her eyes widened slightly but she responded quickly "Are we going to stay here all the afternoon with this nonsense?"

"Perhaps Constable Green can take a look under the stairs before we leave. Please sit down for a moment."

Green needed no bidding and went out to the hallway and opened the door to the under-stair cavity. There was no light in the cupboard so Green had to use his bull nose lamp to illuminate it. The dim light showed the space contained the normal debris that the average household kept in these places. Boxes of ornaments, a spare standard lamp with a partially damaged shade, two stools which did not match the furniture in the parlour and right at the back, a rolled up hearthrug.

Green brought the rug into the parlour, laid it on the floor and unrolled it. There was a large stain which appeared to be blood,

"Would you like to say anything about this rug, Mrs Brunswick?" Morrison asked.

She did not respond.

"Do you still insist that your lodger did not die here in this room and that you knew nothing of it?"

Still no reply.

"Mrs Brunswick, You are an educated lady and must be aware that your continued silence on what took place here will not help you in court. I would surmise that it could go against you if later you attempt to claim that your lodger died as a result of an accident. By then it is unlikely to be believed in the face or your silence now."

"But it was an accident and I am not going to say anything else until I have seen a lawyer."

The local beat constable who alternated with Green was in the square so was dispatched back to the station to advise the inspector and to bring the police van.

Morrison did not pursue the matter any further. Green remained by the parlour door although it seemed unlikely that the woman would attempt to escape.

George decided to use the time in looking around in the other rooms. There had been a search but he had not been involved so was not familiar with the rest of the house. On the same floor as the parlour there was a small room containing a desk and an office type chair. The top of the desk was clear with the exception of of an ornate ink well and some brass knibbed pens in a glass tray. There was a single drawer which was locked. This presented no problem as the key was in the pen tray. The drawer contained only a leather bound desk diary which had very few entries none of which appeared significant. On closing the diary George noticed the corner of a slip of paper protruding from the leather cover. It was a receipt for a deposit at the luggage room and London Bridge station.

They did not have long to wait for the "Black Maria" and returned to the station. The woman was once again placed in the anteroom and Morrison went to report to the inspector. He was not there having decided to go home to his wife and Morrison had to wait to tell him of the success of the expedition.

Morrison wrote up his report of what was found at the house and then asked the sergeant about the next move. There was no doubt that the Inspector needed to be called back to the station as this was going to affect his appearance at the magistrates court in the morning.

"Whilst we wait for the Inspector, you and Evans can go up to the station and see what is being held against that receipt."

George was pleased that the sergeant had made the suggestion as it saved him from going there without instructions. He was back in safe grounds now. He had made a valuable find and perhaps there was more.

Morrison was not surprised to find that handing in the receipt at the station produced a black doctors type bag which were beginning to be called Gladstones. The opened the bag in front of the clerk in order to include him as a witness. The bag contained four large leather pouches containing gold coins, sovereigns. At a guess at least two hundred . Despite the clerks protests, Morrison told him they would take away both the bag and the receipt and that he would no doubt be called to give evidence about what had been found.

Back at the station they found that the Inspector had arrived.

76

The Inspector was ambivalent about being called back to the station and missing his dinner but he had to admit that the constables has done well in producing the evidence which should seal the fate of the Brunswicks. It would not matter a great deal what explanation they produced for the blooded rug and the possession of the coins. They were clearly implicated in the death of the man in the watchhouse and their denials up till then would go against them at the Bailey.

But what to do now. Give them the opportunity to explain or just produce the evidence at the court? See them separately or together?

Mrs. Brunswick had been given no opportunity to advise her husband of the discovery of the rug and neither of them knew that the bag had been recovered from the luggage department at the station.

Well there was time to see them and be home in time for his supper.

"Have you counted those coins, Morrison" he asked when the constable returned to the office.

"Yes sir. Three hundred in all. Sovereigns."

"Genuine, do you think?"

"I don't know, Sir. I have handled too few sovereigns in my life to be able to judge. You may be able to sir, or you may need to call in someone from the mint for an opinion."

"Right, put the bag on the corner of my desk and then bring in Brunswick."

"Just the man, sir?"

"That's what I said. Let's see how he reacts to the bag and then we will shown him the rug"

Brunswick was beginning to show signs of his day and a half at the police station. His clothes were crumpled and unkempt and his face appeared grubby.

He appeared to ignore the bag on the desk and sat when indicated to do so by the inspector.

"What can you tell be about this bag here?"

"Why should I be able to tell you anything about it, Inspector? I have never seen it before."

"I presume then that you have not seen this receipt for it's deposit at the railway station. This receipt that was found secreted in a desk at your home."

"As I said, I have not seen it before."

"Mr. Brunswick. I am not in the mood to play cat and mouse with you. I should be at home instead of here giveing you the opportunity to explain what happened to your lodger. I could send you back to the cells and present our evidence to the Magistrate in the morning. You will be sent to the Old Bailey and will hang shortly thereafter."

"But you have no evidence."

"Mr. Brunswick. That bag is evidence, the clerk at the station will identify you. Your wife has admitted that the man died at your house and his blood has been found there. You are an intelligent man and no doubt read the newspapers. Do you think that a jury would not convict you of the murder of the man just on this evidence alone? I doubt that it would matter what story you and a lawyer may concoct to explain them."

Brannan was amazed by the man's resilience and almost began to doubt that he was involved. But the evidence was too great. It was impossible that the woman could have done it alone.

"I do not believe that my wife has admitted anything of the kind and that bag proves nothing."

"The bag is just one piece of evidence, Mr. Brunswick, there is the blood at your house, there is you wife's admission in front of witnesses. if you cannot see that this would condemn you, then you are a fool."

"What did my wife admit?"

"I cannot tell you that. You are jointly accused and what your wife has said will be attested to in court. Now if you wish to make a statement regarding what occured at your house at the time of his death, then that will be submitted also. Failing that your silence on the subject, despite all the evidence will be submitted instead."

The man did not respond and Brennan said no more. Morrison seated in the corner of the room making notes, wondered how long the silence could last.

Brennan pushed back his chair and stood. "Constable, return this idiot to the cells and in a month he will be in the condemned cell at Newgate."

Brunswick then broke his silence. "I cant be condemned for something I did not do."

Brennan resumed his seat.

"I thought that I had made it clear to you, Mr. Brunswick The evidence shows that you are implicated in the death of your erstwhile lodger. So you will not be condemned for something you have not done. I do not know if in fact you struck the fatal blow that caused his death and it may well be that in the absence of your wife's evidence at the trial then a jury may well believe that you did not. In your shoes I would not like to take a chance on that slim possibility."

"I did not kill him."

"But you do know what happened, because you helped to dispose of the body. It will be too late when you are standing in the dock at the Central Criminal Court to claim that you had no other involvement."

"I did not kill him."

"So you said. But what did you do?"

"As you said, I helped dispose of the body but nothing else."

"So who did kill him?

"My wife said it was an accident. I came home and found him dead in the parlour. My wife was hysterical and could not explain what had happened. There was a storm brewing outside so I went to the kitchen and sent the cook home and decided what to do."

Brennan waited to see if there was going to be more. Apparently not.

"Did your wife later tell you what had happened at the house before you arrived?

"No. She refused to discuss it after we returned home and I decided not to press the matter."

"So where was the body when you first saw it?

"In front of the fireplace and it was apparent he had fallen and struck his head on the fire surround."

"Why did you not call for assistance?"

"There could be no assistance. He was dead."

"Very well, no medical assistance perhaps, but why not call the local constable?

"I told you. My wife was hysterical and insisted that I did not call the police."

"Did she explain why?"

"She thought she would not be believed."

"Did you believe her?"

"Yes of course."

"So why then, did you accept that the police would not do likewise, especially as she had not explained the circumstances?"

"I don't know. I could not think clearly and decided that perhaps the best thing to do was to get the body out of the house and hope that it would not be connected to us."

"And since that time you have not discussed that night with your wife to discover precisely what happened?"

"No. She refused to discuss it. Has she told you?"

"I am not at liberty to say what admissions your wife has made in that connection."

"Well then, you know more than I."

"Did you have any suspicions prior to that night that your lodger may have been making advances to your wife?"

"No. Did she tell you that he had?"

"I am asking what you know Mr. Brunswick."

"Well if he was, then I was not aware of it. As I have told you previously I rarely saw the man and I am sure that if he had been doing what you suggest then my wife would have told me. I would then have shown him the door."

"Did you see anyone on your way from the house to where you left the body?"

"No. It was pouring with rain and there was no one about."

"What did you do with all his personal effects?"

"I thought that if I emptied his pockets then no one would know who he was."

"And this bag?"

i found it in the wardrobe the next day. Saw the coins and did not know what to do. So I deposited them at the station."

"Intending to retrieve them later?"

"I had not thought that far ahead. What are you going to do now, Inspector? You cannot charge me with murder as there was no murder."

"We only have you word for that."

"Then, in the circumstances I will say no more."

Brunswick got up from his chair having regained his composure and turned towards the door."

"Mr. Brunswick. I will remind you that you are a prisoner here and I will tell when this interview is finished."

Brunswick resumed his seat and said nothing.

"You have said that there was no murder and yet you also say that you do not know how he died. How do you reconcile that?"

"I do not attempt to, Inspector and I have told you that I will say no more without a legal representative."

Brennan stood. "What you have told me this afternoon will not alter the charges you will face at the Magistrates court in the morning. Take him away constable."

77

As they sat at their usual table in the chophouse that Sunday evening Frank asked "When do you think that I will be able to get the story from Inspector Brannan then George?"

"Well, you can go and ask him tomorrow after the magistrates hearing. You will get the basic facts at the court and he will perhaps have a mind to fill you in on anything else. But that may well depend on the result of the hearing. As they want a lawyer the magistrate may allow an adjournment for a couple of days."

"So what else is there? The coining business was a red herring all along, wasn't it?"

"I am not sure that I would call it a red herring as such. It was part of the reason why Sylvester was in this division and in a way why he was murdered."

"What do you mean? The woman did it to cover up her background, didn't she?"

"That is my reading of it, yes. But that may not have been the motive and until she tells us, if she ever does, then we can only assume that it was related to her music hall background. But if he hadn't been hiding from Brannan's watchers from the Mint, he would not have come to this side of the river and become entangled with the woman and would probably be alive today. But then again he might not be: he could easily have been at the factory when it blew up."

"All that's assumption" the reporter demurred.

"Of course it is. We have no means of knowing what would have happened if he had not been tipped off that he was being watched and decided to decamp over here. He could have given himself away to the watchers in some way and been arrested and be safely in prison. Or the coining factory could have been shifted away from those arches in Shadwell without the watchers knowing and the investigation could have fizzled out. Don't forget they lost him once before. He could have gone back to Birmingham and we would not have found his body in the watchhouse. All assumptions about what might have been.

He was unlucky that events conspired against him. He expected to get rich being the middle man in the coining by helping to shift large quantities of counterfeits. Instead he ended up on a slab at the morgue."

"He couldn't have got rich shifting even large numbers of half-crowns."

"No, but the half-crowns were a test of the system. They obviously moved onto fake gold coins so the profit and the commission would have been greater. The machine they were using was destroyed in the explosion but it seemed that it was quite capable of producing good quality fakes of any denomination."

The newspaper man liked a good story and was not averse to using guesswork to pad one out but he thought that George was being just a bit fanciful. He tucked the thoughts away but he might still be able to use it later. There was going to be plenty of copy in the weeks to come from the magistrates hearing through to the inevitable trial at the Bailey. There hadn't been a female murderer in Bermondsey since Mrs Manning in 1849 so there was going to be plenty of interest.

"So are we going to get the why of all this at the magistrates or will it all wait till the Bailey?"

"I don't know the answer to that" the constable replied "and in any case which "whys" in particular are you talking about?"

"Well we know she probably killed him to cover up her background or perhaps because he made sexual approaches to her. Or perhaps it really was an accident as she claimed. The husband agreed to help dispose of the body but why put it in the watch-house and how did they do it?"

George grinned "You probably won't believe this but although she did not make a confession I think they intended to dump the body in the river. With no other means available they put it in a perambulator to take it there. On the way, the weight was too much over the cobbles and the wheels buckled. There was a heavy storm, you will no doubt recall, so they stopped at the watchhouse to shelter. Brunswick had a bunch of keys in his pocket and found one to open the padlock. So they put the body inside and pushed the pram around the corner and abandoned it."

"A perambulator?"

"Yes Frank. Quite brilliant really, or it may have been fortuitous as being the only conveyance available. Sylvester was a slight man so fitted into the pram with his legs bent and covered with a shawl. It was a wet afternoon or even later, so who is going to take any notice of a couple hurrying along in the rain pushing a baby's pram?"

"I won't be able to print that." the newspaper man laughed, "No one would believe it."

"You may not have to. Depends on the defence they use after they see a lawyer. With no witnesses apart from the two of them, they can concoct whatever story a lawyer considers is their best option. If you think you are a good storyteller, wait till you hear what they come up with."

Printed in Great Britain
by Amazon